I0691701

Dedication

To anyone who has loved, lost, and learned to love again.

Etched is centered around love and loss and includes frank discussion about the death of a parent, the death of a spouse, murder, and conversation surrounding terminal cancer.

Please exercise care if any of the above may be potentially triggering for you.

Playlist

Damn I Wish I Was Your Lover
-Sophie B. Hawkins

The Lover After You-Savage Garden

Maybe It's Time-Troy Ramey

I Remember Everything-Brandi Carlile

Devil in Her Eyes-Bryce Savage

Days Like This-Dermot Kennedy

One Day at a Time-Jermy Voltz

Both Sides Now-Luke Sital-Singh

If You Ever Wanna Be In Love
-James Bay

Way Down We Go-Stripped
-KALEO

Soldier
-Gavin DeGraw

Colour Me-Juke Ross

You're Gonna Make Me Lonesome
When You Go-Miley Cyrus

Roll Up Your Sleeves-Meg Mac

Have A Little Faith In Me-SYML

Into The Mystic-Andy Kong

Rather Be-Jasmine Thompson

I Think We're Alone Now-The Wild Reeds

Mount Everest-Labrinth

Fare The Well-Oscar Isaac, Marcus Mumford

Wrecking Ball-Patrick Droney

Sweet Love of Mine (Acoustic)
-Joy Williams

Baby Mine-Voctave

Your Song-Ellie Goulding

Lover-The National Parks

Etched

A Broken Sparrow Novel

AMITY MALCOM

One
DAPHNE

THERE ARE A FEW THINGS A PERSON SHOULD KNOW ABOUT having a relationship with their best friend like I have with mine. One, we're not afraid to call each other out. If one of us looks like Shrek trekking through a swamp in the middle of summer, the other will certainly point it out. Two, while we haven't had to, we would absolutely help one another hide a body. I'm not saying we have had detailed conversations about where we would hide said body, but I'm also not saying that we haven't had detailed conversations about where we would hide said body. And three, when one of us is in need, the other will come running. We've been there through everything—from breakups and opening a business together, to new lovers and cross-country moves.

In fact, that's how I find myself in my current situation.

My old SUV is packed solid. Seriously, if you opened the trunk right now, I'm fairly certain you'd be assaulted by an avalanche of boxes, clothes, and old stuffed animals that most women in their mid-thirties would have thrown out years ago.

There is barely enough room in the front of the vehicle for myself in the driver's seat and my best friend, Mina, in the passenger seat. Her long legs are twisted around a small cooler stuffed full of snacks, and the floorboard around her is littered with empty soda bottles, chip bags, and chocolate wrappers that only solidify the fact that we've been in the car for entirely way too long.

"Daph," my bestie says through clenched teeth, "I *really* have to pee."

I flip my sunglasses up on top of my head, peering over at Mina. "Give me a number."

"It's bad."

"Number, Mina."

She lets out a sigh, but I know she loves me.

"On a scale of one to ten, I'm at a solid eight and a half."

We've been on many road trips together over the years, but nothing as massive as driving from Portland all the way across the country to Johnson Creek, a *super* tiny town in North Carolina.

But like I said, Mina and I, we'd truly do anything for one another. So, when she took over an amazing little tattoo shop in her hometown and asked me to move to the middle of nowhere to help her run it, I of course, said yes. Back in Portland, we ran a successful all-female owner shop together, working alongside each other every day to hone our craft and build our brand. Daunting cross-country move aside, I was looking forward to working together daily again.

Mina had moved back to her hometown, Johnson Creek, almost two and a half years ago to help her brother with his teenage daughters after his wife passed away. While she was there, not only did she start working at the amazing shop she now runs, but she fell in love, too—and with her brother's best friend, nonetheless. Seriously, it's like she was plucked from her normal life and placed right into the middle of a romance novel.

The lucky bitch.

Eyes on the road, I pass a sign for an upcoming rest stop. Mina sees it too and quickly points it out. "Swear to God and all things holy, if you do not pull over up ahead, I will pee in your seat."

"One, that's fucking disgusting. Two, you're the one who would have to sit in it."

She rolls her eyes at me so dramatically that I'm pretty sure she sees her brain.

"I'll stop," I tell her. "But only because I really want a soft pretzel and the rest stop food courts always have the best."

Laughing, she turns to me the best she can in the seat. "You'd really let me pee in your car seat?"

"Listen, I just want to get there. I feel like we've been in this car for fucking days, and every time we stop, it sets us back even further."

Mina offers to swap driving duties with me after the rest stop, and I consider for all of point three seconds before turning her down. At a solid five foot nothing, I can't stand letting other people drive my SUV. It takes days for me to get the seat back exactly the way I like it, and don't even get me started on the fucking mirrors. Let me tell you, it's a nightmare.

If I'm lucky—which I'm usually not—this will be our last stop before we cruise into the cute-ass, little town I'm about to call home.

My best friend's phone cuts into our nineties music playlist, and she reaches over to turn the volume down before pressing the phone to her ear. As soon as she hears the voice on the other end, a huge smile engulfs her face, and I know it's her now husband—her brother's best friend—Nico.

All too quickly, her smile fades as she makes a few noncommittal groans, grunts, and sighs. Honestly, when the two of them are together, they can have an entire conversation through random glances and noises. It's sickeningly sweet, but I'd be lying if I said I don't crave the type of closeness she has with her husband.

She hangs up a few minutes later, throwing a cautious glance in my direction.

"Do I even want to know?" I ask her, absolutely wanting to know.

"There has been a *slight* change of plans."

"Mina, so help me God, if you tell me to turn this car around and drive back to Portland, I may just actually lose my fucking mind."

"No, no, no. It's nothing like that," she reassures me through a grimace. "Nico said the contractor hit a pipe when they were demoing a wall between rooms and flooded the entire wing of the house where you were going to be staying. Apparently, it's a mess and going to take way more time than we originally planned to get it fixed."

I gasp, half horrified for myself, half horrified for the gorgeous Victorian house that Mina and Nico have been restoring for the last two years. The place is massive, way more space than any two people need, but they've been painstakingly working at it, doing most of the work themselves, with hopes of one day filling it with lots of children.

"The one time you guys hire out someone to do the work."

She nods solemnly. "But don't worry, Nico spoke with Colin, and he said you're more than welcome to stay with him until our place is ready or you find your own place."

Eyes widening, I look at Mina a second too long before bringing my eyes back to the road in front of us. "You want me to stay with your brother?"

Trust me, I have no problem staying with Colin. Except for

the fact that he shares his home with two teenagers and a rambunctious dog. I don't do kids. Or animals. It's not that they don't like me; for some odd reason they always do. It's just that I don't really like them. Both species are dirty, loud, and are almost always sticky for some reason or another. Then again, I bet most of my ex-boyfriends would say the same about me.

And then, there is Colin.

I've only had the pleasure of meeting him three times in all the years I've known Mina, all three happening since she returned to Johnson Creek. And each time, I've found myself wildly attracted to the older man, who, for all intents and purposes can only be described as having a stick shoved so far up his ass that it could come out of his mouth at any time.

When I say he is serious, I mean he is *serious*. I don't think I've ever truly seen the man smile. Not when he interacts with his mother or when he's hanging out with his best friend. Hell, I don't think he even had a true smile on his face when he escorted his sister down the aisle on her wedding day.

He's the extreme opposite of his sister. Of his best friend. Of me.

But man, do I want to ruffle his perfectly coiffed hair and wrinkle his perfectly pressed monogrammed dress shirts that everyone relentlessly teases him about.

They say that opposites attract, and as cliché as that sounds, I'd like nothing more than to attract that man to my bed. Which, apparently, is going to be in his house for the fore-seeable future.

I snap back to Mina after hearing her snapping my name. "What? Sorry, I was just thinking of everything I need to finalize when we get there on top of the prospect of living with your smoking hot brother."

She laughs, rolling her eyes at me. "I said that now that my mom isn't there anymore, you'll have the second primary suite, so it's almost like having your own house. You'll barely even have to see him if you don't want to. Plus, with his work schedule, he's barely home anyways."

Here's the thing though—I *want* to see Colin. I've wanted to see him again since the very first time I laid eyes on him over a phone screen as Mina sat sandwiched on his kitchen floor between him and Nico after a scary experience with her stalker ex-boyfriend.

Ever since that day, I've wanted to run my fingers through his slightly cropped, inky black hair, which was streaked with the slightest amount of gray. I've wanted to stare deep into his green eyes, so very similar to his sister's yet nothing alike. I've wanted to climb his tall, muscular frame and wrap my legs around his waist as I pressed my lips to his. I've even wanted to find the secret tattoo he hides somewhere on his body and run my tongue over it, not caring where it is or what the design is of.

Yet with all those wants, there is one thing I would absolutely, never in a million years, do, and that's act on them. Sure, Mina may have found love with her brother's best friend, but certainly, as the old adage goes, lightning never strikes the same place twice.

For me, that's a fucking shame because that man is nothing short of tasty with a capital T.

And so far out of my league that we're basically not even in the same solar system.

He's beautiful and refined, while I'm slightly shaggy and rough around the edges. Hell, he probably knows which fork to start with at fancy dinner parties, while I'd surely make a fool out of myself. I'm a tattoo artist who spends my days around a rag-tag bunch of characters, wielding my tattoo machine and permanently etching designs on people's skin, while he spends his day as an attorney, helping underrepresented groups fighting for basic rights in family court. He's a hero to so many, while I'm just a silly, little girl trying to make enough to carve out a decent living for myself.

Colin's cautious, whereas I'm curious.

He's organized, and I'm a fucking mess.

He's shy and reserved, while I love to be the life of the party.

Surely, he's vanilla as they come while I've never met a kink I didn't like.

And starting later today, he's going to be my new roommate.

So help us all, this is going to be a fucking nightmare.

Two

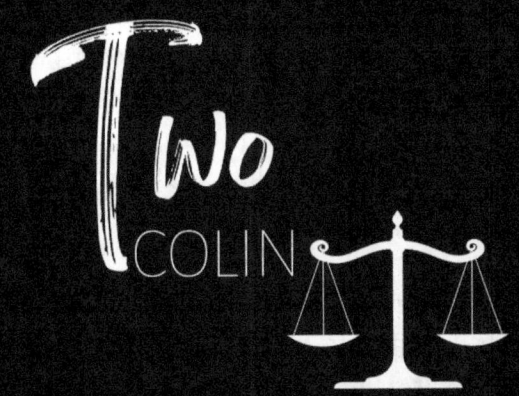

COLIN

I'm not sure exactly when it happened, when I woke up one morning to find that more than half of my life had passed me by, but as I stand here in front of the bathroom vanity, looking at the man staring back at me, I only have one thought.

When did I get so *old*?

Hair that once used to be jet black now has more gray than it did only a few short years ago. I have noticeable bags under my eyes from lack of sleep, and I momentarily think to myself that maybe it is time to start a skincare routine much like my sister has been recommending. Even the light coating of hair that covers my chest has transitioned. It's only a matter of time before I have to start plucking hairs from my ears, and my daughters start buying me nose hair trimmers for the holidays.

Thankfully, I still have a half-decent body thanks to a rigorous morning workout routine. Used partially to keep myself in shape to keep up with my girls, I also use the converted garage-turned-gym as a place to find myself after long days in court, where I advocate for men and women who have often been taken advantage of throughout their lives.

To say I'm at a much different place in my life than I thought I would be at forty-five is an understatement. Yes, I have two gorgeous daughters, an adorable yet slightly senile dog who sometimes pees on the floor, a fantastic family, and a steady, fulfilling yet demanding job, but there is one thing missing.

Tabitha.

Pulling my gaze from my reflection, I walk from the attached bathroom into my bedroom, rubbing the ring that encircles my left ring finger. It's a habit I've had since the day my wife placed it on that very finger, a habit that even now, nearly two and a half years since she left us, that I still do on a subconscious level multiple times each day. I find myself rubbing that spot when I'm anxious, when I'm stressed, and especially when I think back on the memories I shared with my beautiful wife. To be honest, it's a miracle I haven't rubbed straight through the thin metal.

I hate that after all this time, I can still feel stinging at the back of my eyes when I think of my late wife. That every day I wake up and the grief is just as fresh as it was the day we got her cancer diagnosis. As raw as it was when we decided to stop treatment and seek comfort care, and as all-encompassing as it was on the day she took her last breath.

Thinking you have forever to spend with someone and actually having forever are certainly two very different things. At least today, when I think about her, the tears that threaten to fall choose to stay locked away, instead only prickling to escape.

Downstairs, I hear the door slam, bringing me out of the fog of memories started by the lavender-vanilla-scented candle that was always burning in our room. Now, there is an unburned version of the same candle sitting atop my dresser, a reminder of the life I shared with the woman I loved. I don't dare burn it, the fear of knowing I would be extinguishing a tiny bit of Tabitha's memory every time I blow it out is simply too much to bear.

"Yoo hoo, brother! I brought you your new roomie!"

I run a hand over the scruff that lines my jaw, trying to push down my emotions before walking downstairs to greet my sister and her best friend. Just one case in point to thinking my life would be different at my age. Today, while in my dreams, I'd be spending the day with my beautiful wife, the woman I thought I'd have forever with in our dream house, I have a roommate moving in instead.

Of course, this isn't a roommate in the traditional sense of the word. For starters, we're not actually sharing a room, but an entire house. And for that, I'm thankful.

It isn't that I wouldn't do anything for my sister—I absolutely would. That includes letting her best friend crash with me and my girls because the room she was going to be staying in with Mina and Nico is currently under a solid six inches of standing water.

But Mina's friend, Daphne...well, she's a bit of a loose cannon.

I've never met a woman who curses as freely as she does, her colorful words enough to make me blush at times. She's crass, saying what's on her mind even when it is highly inappropriate, and even though she is in her thirties, she dresses like she's my seventeen-year-old daughter's age—my seventeen-year-old daughter, who I am *always* trying to get to cover up more of herself.

I'd be lying if I said I wasn't slightly concerned about the influence she will hold over Emily and Laurel, but even more so, I'm worried about the influence she will have on my own life.

When I said I had a strong family support system, I meant it. Directly after Tabitha's death, my mother moved in with me and my girls, only moving out a few months ago and into a condo ten short minutes away. And shortly after, when I still needed more support than I had on hand, my sister left her life in Portland to move back home, living with me until she fell in love with and subsequently moved in with my best friend.

Talk about a wild ride.

But aside from the two adult women who mean the most to me and my two beautiful daughters, there has been no female influence in my home. Nothing to remove Tabitha's presence, her little touches like oversized throw pillows on the cream-colored couch or the family photos as our girls grew up lining the stairs that turned this house into a home. And that's exactly the way I like it.

I don't want to erase her memory from this house any more than I want to erase her memory from my mind, and it terrifies me that having a woman in this space will do exactly that.

Feeling the cold floor under my bare feet, I make my way down the hardwood steps, pausing only briefly to look at the pictures of the happy family that stare back at me. I can see my girls growing up in the pictures, the most recent one taken just weeks before Tabitha passed. In the picture, she sits in a hospital bed, propped up by several pillows, with no trace of her once long, copper hair in sight. A stylish wrap adorns her bald head, a gentle smile on her lips as her blue eyes seemingly look through the camera and right into the soul of anyone who looks at the picture. We're all crowded on the bed with her, arms wrapped around her in a showing of love. It simultaneously fills me with joy and breaks my heart every time I look at it.

Barreling toward the noise of what will surely be chaos, I mentally remind myself that this is only temporary. A few weeks at most and I'll be back to my peaceful existence–just me, my daughters, and the world's most ornery old dog.

"Colin!" Daphne launches herself into my arms, squeezing me tightly. I stiffen under the unexpected touch, not because I've only met the woman in person a few times, but because I'm simply not sure how to respond to the feel of a woman so closely pressed against my chest.

I settle for a gentle pat on the back before I make quick work of extracting myself from her embrace. If it bothers her that I've cut our contact short, she doesn't let on. "Thank you *so* much for letting me crash. Promise you won't even know I'm here!"

Somehow, I doubt that.

She hoists an oversized bag I didn't previously see over her shoulder as I give my sister a quick welcome-back hug. Pointing toward the rear of the house, I offer to show her where she'll be staying before helping to bring box after box after box of her belongings into the house.

One of the features that originally sold Tabitha and I on the property I live in was two primary-bedroom suites. With one upstairs and one down, it was the ideal way to give us a bit of privacy while the girls were growing. Only after she passed and my mom moved in did I move to the upstairs suite, giving my mom the opportunity to take the downstairs bedroom. Young for her age, I still didn't want her to have the hassle of climbing stairs multiple times each day. Plus, it gave me the chance to be closer to the girls when nightmares plagued their dreams after their mom's death. Thankfully, as the years passed, those bad dreams have become few and far between for the girls. Me, I'm often a different story.

I bring another box into what is now Daphne's room, stacking it on top of several others that have begun to clutter the corner. Setting it down, I wipe my brow with the hem of my shirt, the sweat of the late spring morning clinging to my skin. "You've got bricks in these or what?"

Daphne scampers across the room like a happy little kitten, tearing open the box. "Nope, just books! Lots and lots of the best romance books ever written."

As she pulls colorful paperbacks from the box, placing them on the quilt that covers the bed, Mina enters the room, arms full of stuffed animals that look like they belong in a little girl's room, not the bedroom of a grown woman.

"Girl, stop unpacking boxes and help unpack the car first!" She tosses a stuffed toy at her friend, who bats it away.

"I just hate boxes. They make me feel so damn unsettled."

My sister crosses the room and rubs small circles on Daphne's back. It reminds me of the circles Tabitha used to draw on our daughter's backs after a feeding or before bed. "I know, babe, and I'm sorry that our original plans didn't work out. But as soon as the house is fixed, we'll move you in, and you'll be able to stay as long as you need."

Exiting the room, wanting to give them privacy, I'm on my way back to the SUV for another load of boxes when I overhear Mina speaking softly. "I know being here means you have to hide a lot of yourself, but thank you, Daphne. Truly, there is no one else I would want to help me with this transition than you."

I can't be sure, but I think I hear the faint sound of sniffles as I walk away, and while I've become an expert in calming teenage tears, I'm nowhere near ready to touch what's happening in that room with a ten-foot pole. Instead, I focus on loading the dolly with boxes, pulling them from the oversized trunk of the SUV and stacking them higher than I should but managing to empty the rest of the vehicle in one load.

Laughter echoes through the house when I re-enter, letting me know it's clear to proceed into the room. I drop off the boxes, quickly looking around the room at the kaleidoscope of colors that up until an hour ago held nothing but a bed and some empty furniture, before heading to the kitchen, pouring myself a glass of iced tea. Finishing the glass, I rinse it before placing it gently in the dishwasher.

Coming up behind me, my sister wraps her arms around my torso. "I'm going to run home for a bit and get the road trip smell off of me, but I'll be back in a couple hours. Promise you'll be nice to her?"

I let out a gruff laugh that startles her. "When am I not nice?"

My sister sighs, looking at me sharply. "Just...she's been through a lot, Colin."

Mina gives me one more hug, promising to be back for dinner, before leaving me alone in the kitchen, wondering exactly what Daphne has been through that has my sister protecting her so fiercely.

Three

DAPHNE

Despite Johnson Creek having a population of just a few thousand people, Broken Sparrow is more than double the size of the tattoo shop Mina and I co-own in Portland. Our successful shop still stands in the Rose City, left in the capable hands of our dedicated staff while she and I are across the country putting our unique spin on our new highly sought-after location.

The shop, as most shops do, smells like home to me with its notes of antiseptic wafting around the space. You can add as many candles, diffusers, or air fresheners to the shop as you want, but you'll never be able to get away from the underlying scent of cleanliness. Some people might say that it smells like a doctor's office or a hospital—almost medicinal—but to me, it is vastly different and fully comforting.

Mina and I are tucked away in the office as tattoo machines whir in the distance, a gentle, calming noise that could lull me to sleep at night. Together, we stand over her desk, looking through paint samples and cabinet colors, flooring choices, and upgraded shop equipment.

Buying Broken Sparrow wasn't something we hastily ran into, and we spent many late nights that turned into early mornings over Facetime working through the pros and cons of branching off of our Portland location, but ultimately, once everything was said and done, all the options laid out, it was an easy decision to make. The shop has been in existence for generations, Mina and I being the first people outside of the family to own Broken Sparrow. Owned by the same family since the shop opened, Mina started at Broken Sparrow as a guest artist when she first came back to Johnson Creek before making it her permanent shop. When the previous owner, Thom, decided it was time to retire, he approached Mina about purchasing the location. It was an honor that they trusted us with their baby, trusted that we would take care of it in the very way we would take care of a member of our own family.

"If I had it my way, I'd paint the entire place pink from floor to ceiling. We could do one of those super cool epoxy floors with glitter in it, bubblegum pink walls, and a mirrored ceiling so clients could see their work as it was happening."

My friend takes a large gulp from her insulated coffee cup before hitting me with a pointed stare. "That is absolutely not happening."

I give her a shrug. "You've gotta admit, it would be pretty fucking cool though."

"Honestly, I don't hate the idea of the glitter floor."

Squealing, I throw my arms around my best friend. "You *do* love me!"

We break into a fit of giggles, something we do so easily and so frequently when we're together. In fact, everything between us is easy. It's part of what makes our friendship so effortless and just a sliver of what makes me love Mina to the moon and back.

She hugs me back, and warmth spreads through my body in her embrace. "There isn't anyone I'd rather be doing this with than you. I'm so glad you made the decision to come."

I'm happy I made that decision too, and I tell her as much while not letting her go.

"Shit, am I interrupting girl time?" John, one of the artists from the shop, comes into the office, stopping in his steps when he sees us embracing. It only serves to have us laughing all over again as we ensure him that he isn't interrupting anything.

After we finally calm down, he tells us the contractor we're looking at hiring is here, and we spend much of the afternoon going over details for the new layout of the shop along with the timeline, and of course, the financial details, too. One of the benefits of Mina marrying a real estate agent is that he has a large network of people he has gotten to know over the years. From contractors and painters to interior designers and custom woodworkers, he has the hookup and has promised to help us do this as financially responsible as possible.

And thank God for that because this shit is expensive.

We'll be tossing dollar bills and making it rain all over the place–metaphorically speaking, of course.

It's not a complete overhaul of the shop, but we will be closing for at least two weeks. Tomorrow is our last day before the renovation, and while we don't have clients scheduled, all our staff offered to come in and help remove the existing fixtures, merchandise, backstock, and art that peppers the walls. Thankfully, in our line of work, many artists travel to do guest spots at various shops around the world, so while we're closed, our artists will still be making money. Raven, our receptionist and overall badass, will be working from home, handling future appointments and social media, and while I could fly back to Portland while we're closed, I'd rather stay in Johnson Creek. Especially after just getting here a few days ago.

Besides, this will give me the perfect excuse to work on unpacking the boxes currently cluttering my room and giving me major anxiety. Don't get me wrong, even with my boxes, the room is spacious. A generous walk-in closet for all my clothes, an empty dresser and nightstands, and an attached bathroom twice the size of the one in my apartment. Hell, I've never even had my own bathroom before, and the thought of soaking in the oversized tub sounds beyond amazing.

Arriving back at Colin's house, I let myself in through the front door, the key he gave me dangling from a Keep Portland Weird keychain. The sound of the keys clinking together on their ring is drowned out by the sounds of Colin and his girls in the kitchen. For all of what Colin has been through, what he and his family have experienced, there is never a lack of laughter when the trio is together.

Walking into the kitchen, I find Colin standing by the oven as the girls measure and pour various ingredients into bowls scattered across the kitchen island. Both teens greet me with cheerful smiles while Colin gives me a single, curt nod. That's the thing about Colin. As friendly and happy as he seems with his girls, when almost anyone else is around, he's serious, a no-nonsense type of guy.

It's something that I never noticed before, but perhaps that was because I had only ever seen him in group settings or because we've only met a handful of times. It's almost like he feels the need to keep an air of apathy for fear of letting any emotion show when he's around others.

I wonder briefly what he was like before his wife passed–if he laughed more around other people, if he shared smiles more freely.

"Wanna help us bake cookies?" Emily asks, wiping some stray flour from her nose.

Laurel, the older of the two, holds up a bag of chocolate chips and shakes them a bit before dumping them into her mixing bowl. She doesn't bother to measure them out, simply drops the contents of the bag. She's totally my type of kid.

It's only been a few days since I moved in, and while I'm not usually one to worry about making waves, I know that Colin is a particular type of man. The type who likes order. Who apparently likes routine.

I look to Colin for guidance. He must see my hesitation because he gives me a small, rare grin that doesn't quite reach his eyes before speaking. It's almost as if he enjoys me asking his permission, even if I did so with just a silent look. "Daphne might be tired from her day, but if not, she's more than welcome to join us."

While I'm thankful for the out, I don't take it. Surprising myself, I find that I want to spend time with Colin's girls, that I want to get to know them. Their giggles are infectious, they have more energy than newborn puppies, and besides–who doesn't love warm cookies fresh from the oven?

"Give me five to get changed, and I'm all yours."

I head toward my room, hearing Colin excuse himself from the kitchen before his footsteps retreat up the stairs. In my room, I throw my hair on top of my head in a messy bun, missing a few strands of hair but not caring. Pulling off my skinny jeans and tight tank, I toss them on the floor before pulling on a pair of sleep shorts and a loose camisole. With my next to nothing breasts, I opt to skip a bra, hating the way they make me feel restricted.

Slipping my feet into a pair of fluffy slippers that always make me feel like a happy kid, I'm about to walk to the kitchen when a knock sounds at the very door I'm turning to open. I reach for the knob, a slow creak echoing throughout my room as I open it to find Colin on the other side.

"Can I talk to you for a second?" His face looks almost pained, like whatever is about to come out of his mouth is certainly something I'm not going to like. It's a far cry from the almost smile I saw just minutes ago.

I give him a little nod, the bun on top of my head bouncing with the movement. Walking into the room, he quietly closes the door behind us, and I suddenly feel trapped.

While most people tower over me by at least a few inches, Colin hovers over a foot taller than me, his size seeming to suck the air from the room. He's in a simple pair of navy joggers and a gray Henley and I can't help but follow the slope of his biceps as they strain against the fabric of the shirt.

He's the type of man that should grace the cover of romance novels, all strong and broad. Muscly without being huge. I'm confident he would look just as good without his shirt as he does with it on.

My gaze continues down his strong arms, lingering on the thick, corded forearms peeking out from his pushed-up sleeves that flow into equally strong, adept hands. Only when my eyes lock on his hands do I notice that one of them is clenched tightly into a fist.

He stares at me for several tense seconds, and I desperately want him to say whatever he has to say to me. To get it over with so we can go about our night, and I can get to eating warm cookies.

"You wanted to talk to me about something?" My voice is small, almost weak when I ask. Him being here, in my room with me, makes me nervous. I'm afraid of what he'll see when he looks around at the boxes still in various degrees of being unpacked, afraid of what he'll see when he looks at me.

Colin takes a step toward me, and I instinctively step back.

A deep crease forms between his brows. Instead of stepping closer, he reaches out his hand, fist still clenched so tightly that his knuckles have begun to turn white.

"You know you are more than welcome here, that you have free rein of anything you need. But can you please be careful with such delicate things as these?"

He opens his palm, a pair of my very tiny, very ruffly, light pink panties dangling from between his fingers. They must have gotten stuck in the washer or dryer when I was doing my wash yesterday. I suck in a sharp breath, my face heating to an almost molten temperature. Embarrassment blooms throughout my body, the flush from my face quickly spreading down my neck and across my chest.

I don't speak as I reach out and gently try to take the thin fabric from between his fingers, my eyes bouncing around the room, looking anywhere but at him. He holds firm, not letting me take my underwear, which prompts me to finally meet his eyes.

"I want you to be comfortable here. I just don't think these are the types of things my daughters need to be seeing at their age. Although, these do look more like something a little girl would wear than a grown woman."

He's not wrong though. They are panties that a little girl would wear, and that's exactly why I like them. They make me feel special, like a little girl who deserves love and attention, not like a thirty-something-year-old woman who has been left alone more times in her life than she can count. Although right here, under Colin's watchful gaze, I don't feel loved or adored. All I feel is shame.

Dropping the underwear into my hand, his fingers lightly graze mine. I'm not sure if it is intentional or not, but knowing Colin, I chalk it up to an accident. Still, I can't stop my breath from hitching as a small zap of electricity radiates out from where his fingers touched me.

Almost as quickly as the shame spread across my body, it's replaced with want, with need and desire that pools low in my belly. I step back, putting more space between us, suddenly even more nervous of being so close to this giant of a man. His eyes are still fixed on me in an unreadable expression, and though I don't dare do it, I want to reach out and touch him. My fingers itch to push the stray hairs back from his face, to run over his scruff, to trace the bow of his upper lip.

"Just, be careful, okay?" His voice is lower when he speaks, like a back road covered in gravel. It's authoritative and a bit rough, like a daddy disciplining a child. The same heat in my belly spreads further south, dampening the panties I'm wearing now that are not frilly or ruffly. It's not meant to be a warning or a command, but my body takes it as so, and I speak before I think better of it.

"Are you going to punish me if I'm not?"

His cheeks flush, like now I'm the one embarrassing him, and it brings me a silly sense of pride that maybe I was able to throw him even just an iota off balance.

A small voice calls from outside the room, both of our gazes snapping to the door. "I...uh, I should get back out there before they burn the house down."

Colin retreats, silently closing the door behind him. I'm going to have to ask him how he does it because the squeak it makes for me is annoying as hell.

I toss the frilly panties on my bed, taking several deep breaths to center myself. And when I finally feel slightly less than frazzled over my interaction with Colin, I open my door with a smile on my face and head to the kitchen, ready to eat my weight in cookies.

Four

COLIN

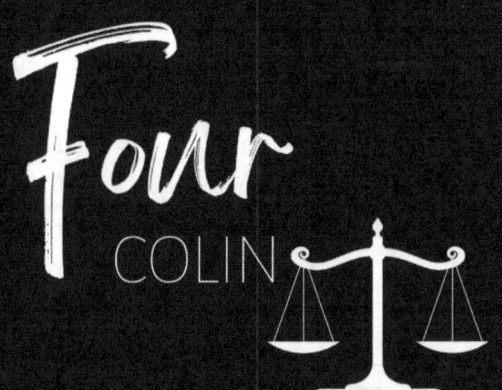

For as long as I can remember, Friday night has been family dinner night. Starting when we were children, my mom insisted we spend each Friday crowded around our little kitchen table, sharing homemade food and stories of our week. Even when I became a teen, while most other boys my age were out partying and chasing girls, I still never missed a Friday family dinner. It was routine; it was safe and familiar, and everything I love about being with family.

Over the years, the number of people has varied—my sister leaving for college, the addition of Tabitha as first my girlfriend and then my wife, my girls, the loss of my father, the loss of my wife—but the tradition has carried on.

Even now, as I push open the door after an exhaustive day at my office, I'm not surprised to find my mom already hard at work, bent over the six-burner stove as she stirs several large, silver pots that rest atop our gas range.

The smell of oregano and basil hangs heavy in the air, my mouth watering at the scent. While my mother has always been known for her delectable Greek dishes, she recently took up cooking classes after moving out of my house, and now, we're treated to a rotating menu of cuisine. Everything from our family's traditional Greek favorites to homemade pierogies, tamales, and tonight, homemade pasta and sauce.

I pull my mom into a hug, her only pausing her constant stirring long enough to give me a quick squeeze. Taking in a deep lungful of the mouthwatering aroma, I over-exaggerate as I cock an eyebrow toward the stove. "Smells great in here."

She lifts a wooden spoon to my lips, urging me to taste the sauce that has been simmering on the stove. At the kitchen island, the girls work in tandem, chopping vegetables for a large garden salad and I can just make out garlic knots through the frosted pane of the oven's window. "Italian tonight. Wait till you try these homemade meatballs. I really think that I was born into the wrong nationality."

Laughter filters into the house as Mina and Daphne walk through the front door together, their conversation flitting back and forth faster than the wings of a hummingbird. I swear, that pair of women could spend every waking moment together and never run out of things to say to one another.

I've never had that feeling with someone before. Not even with my best friend. Not even with my wife.

Sure, Tabitha and I spent time together, and there was always laughter, but we still enjoyed our quiet moments just as much. We spent many nights together in bed or on the couch or on loungers in the backyard, each reading our own books we borrowed from our little town's library.

"Mama P!" Daphne calls out. "I always loved Fridays, but even more so now that I have you to look forward to every week."

My mom huffs in response. "Child, I know you're only

excited for the food I cook. And it looks like it's a good thing you're here. You're practically skin and bone."

Growing up, my mother wasn't necessarily strict with my sister and me—that was always more of my father's job—but she has always been reserved. Yet, despite the night and day differences between her temperate and controlled attitude and Daphne's loud and sometimes crass counterpart, the two women get along surprisingly well.

Daphne giggles in response, grabbing a cucumber slice from the wooden cutting board on the counter and popping it into her mouth. She speaks with a full mouth. "You do yourself a great disservice if you think I'm only here for your cooking and your ability to make me gain five pounds just from looking at a plate of food. While a huge motivating factor, it's really that shining personality of yours that I love."

My mom lets out a low chuckle as my sister trails Daphne off to her bedroom.

Nico is the last to arrive, and once he does, everyone reconvenes around the large, glass-top table in the backyard. Overflowing bowls are passed around, the scents hanging in the air along with the unseasonably late-spring humidity while Stella hides under the table, waiting for any small scrap to fall.

"Daddy?" Laurel's voice pipes up as I'm about to take my first bite of salad. Jesus, when was the last time she called me daddy? At seventeen, it seems like it has been years, and even though she is morphing into more and more of a woman every day, she sounds every bit like the little girl I remember from all those years ago.

I look across the table to find her big, blue eyes—the spitting image of her mother—looking back at me.

But being a father to two teenage girls has taught me a thing or two and from her tone, I know she's about to ask for something.

"Prom is in a few weeks and I still need to get a dress. A bunch of the girls from school are going next weekend with their moms. I was thinking maybe Aunt Mina and Daphne could go with me since Mom isn't here for it."

My heart breaks for my girl, for another moment she will never be able to share with her mother. Doing my best to hide my emotion from my voice and face, I give her a nod and force a smile. "If they have the time and it isn't an inconvenience to them."

"Are you kidding me? I'd love to!" my sister says at the same time Daphne says, "This is why we own the business, so we can be there for family when we're needed."

Family.

Growing up, we're taught family is blood. Those people who are the very essence of our beings are the people to lean on, to trust, to share in your hopes and dreams. And while that is true, over the last two and a half years, I've learned that family is so much more than flesh and blood.

Family is the partners at my law office, who were there for me every step of the way after Tabitha's death, taking on my caseload when I was too distraught to pull myself out of bed, let alone to be there for my clients. They brought me meals, cleaned my house, and even cut my lawn in the weeks following her passing.

Family is my best friend sitting to my left at this table—Nico, the man who literally pulled me out of the aforementioned bed, forcing me into the shower after almost two weeks without one, and helping me to show up for my daughters, who were experiencing grief in their own, young ways. Those days were dark, yet time and time again, he showed up for me, talked me into seeking therapy, and even sat with me on this very porch as I cried inconsolably.

And now, by some odd cosmic intervention, Daphne is

slowly beginning to transform into family, too. Of course, my sister has loved her for years, but now, my daughters do, too. I've caught tender moments as she sneaks up the stairs each night, popping her head into both of their rooms to say good-night. She's helped Emily with her hair and makeup when my kid complained she didn't have anything that was "grown-up" enough for a fourteen-year-old, and she has spent time indulging the girls while watching their favorite Netflix shows, nestled between them on the couch while balancing a huge bowl of popcorn on her lap. Daphne has even picked up after Stella when she has had accidents, something she absolutely did not sign up for. Last week, as I walked down to Daphne's room to drop off yet another pair of frilly underwear that was left behind in the washer, I even caught the old dog cuddling up at the foot of her bed while the little pixie slept soundly under a colorful, tattered quilt.

It's been unexpected how well she has become part of our day-to-day routine and surprisingly, I don't hate it.

In fact, I actually kind of like it.

Over our meal, the girls get lost in conversations about dresses. Words like tulle and taffeta are being thrown around while they talk about color, silhouette, and length. Even my mom chimes in with her opinion, sending the rest of them careening down another prom-focused tangent.

Nico and I both eye the influx of estrogen ping-ponging around the table before looking toward the house.

"Drink in my office?" I ask.

"Thought you'd never ask. I was starting to sweat from all this," he responds, waving his hand in the general direction of the women sitting around the table.

We sneak inside the house, the girls none the wiser to our departure, and take up residence in the small home office I keep on the ground floor. Settling into the chair behind my desk, I open a cabinet, producing a bottle of scotch and two glasses.

I pour a few fingers in each of the crystal glasses, a wedding present from Tabitha's parents, before taking a healthy swig of the warm, amber liquid. It heats my throat as it travels further down before settling low in my stomach.

My friend eyes me suspiciously over the rim of his own glass, unaccustomed to seeing me down hard liquor so quickly.

"So, that was...a lot," Nico says before joining me, slamming down half his glass.

Nodding in agreement, I sigh before my head falls back against my leather office chair.

"How's it been going, having your houseguest here?"

"Surprisingly, not nearly as horrible as I expected it to be. I mean, she's still infuriating at times, listens to the weirdest music ever, and has a tendency to always leave a pair or two of little panties in the washer..."

Nico snorts at the last part. "Do you think she does it on purpose?"

I rub a palm over the scruff on my face. "Honestly, I have no idea. Regardless, she gets along so well with the girls. She helps them with homework, gives them advice when they ask for it, and never treats them like they are too young to hang out with her. Hell, sometimes, I feel like she is almost more comfortable with two teenagers than she is with me—someone just a few years older than she is. There is one thing that bothers me though."

My friend raises an inquisitive brow in my direction.

Reaching for the bottle, I pour another helping into each of our glasses.

"The day she moved in, I overheard my sister tell Daphne that she knew the woman had to hide herself being in my house, and then, before she left, she told me that I needed to be nice, that Daphne had been through a lot. I just, I don't know what it is that she thinks she has to hide."

Nico downs his glass, not meeting my eyes.

So much for two gentlemen enjoying an after-dinner drink like two adults. At this pace, we'll both be drunk within the next half hour.

"You know what it is, don't you?"

"Colin, I am begging you, don't make me tell you."

"How bad can it be?"

My friend lets out a long sigh. "You're like a brother to me, Colin. My poor, innocent, vanilla brother."

"What, you're saying she's into...like...whips and chains and stuff?"

Nico snorts. "Not that I'm aware of."

"So just tell me. I've seen *Fifty Shades*. How bad can it be?"

Although it's just the two of us in the office, he lowers his voice and leans across my desk. "She's a *little*."

"Yeah, I know. She's really tiny."

"Dude, no." My best friend takes off his glasses and runs his hands over his face. "I mean, she *is* tiny, but that's not what I'm saying. She gets off on having someone treat her like a child. Calling someone *Daddy*. Doing activities that someone younger generally participates in. That kind of thing."

My face must show my shock. I have heard of women calling men Daddy before, but I always assumed it was just something that happened in the movies. "I'm truly terrified to ask how you know this. Please tell me that my sister doesn't call you *Daddy*?"

A grin stretches across his face as he goes to speak, but I cut him off. "Wait, I do not want to know the answer to that."

"I've just overheard Mina talking to her about it a few times. Those two couldn't be discrete if their lives depended on it." The sentiment is solidified by the sounds of whooping laughter as the women begin to bring in leftovers and dishes.

Dropping his voice again, knowing everyone has returned to the house, Nico continues. "She had a pretty serious relationship in Portland, had been with the guy for a few years, but found out he was sharing photos she sent him with other men online. Charging them to see the racier ones and racking himself up quite a little nest egg."

My mind is spinning as I try to take in all the information Nico shared with me. The hurt and pain she must have felt at her ex's betrayal, the humiliation of being put in that position by someone you trust. I want to seek her out right now, wrap her in a hug and tell her how sorry I am that she had to experience such a horrible invasion of her privacy.

I find myself wanting to pull her into my arms, wanting to tell her that I'll take care of her and that I can be whatever she needs me to be because no one should feel that pain. It's an odd sensation, one I haven't felt in over two years.

My sister pokes her head into the office, stopping our conversation as she asks her husband if he is ready to leave. We follow her to the kitchen, where they load up their arms with plastic containers full of leftovers. My mother has never known how to cook for any party size less than twenty, and it shows each Friday evening.

I send my mom home next before she tries to do the remaining dishes, and soon after, the girls get picked up to head to a friend's house for a Friday night sleepover.

Daphne reenters the kitchen a short time later, picking up a dishrag to dry the dishes I've been setting on the counter. She's changed into pajamas, a silky little set that leaves little to the imagination, the outline of her pert, little nipples pressing against the thin fabric. Her face is free of makeup, her long hair tied up on top of her head, and an always present pair of fuzzy slippers on her feet.

We work in a comfortable silence, me washing while she dries, making quick work of the pile of dishes needed to feed seven people and one beggar of a dog.

When the last of the dishes are put away, she replaces her towel over the handle of the oven. She's almost out of the kitchen when I call out to her, the tiny slipper clad feet propelling her toward her room coming to a stop.

"Thank you for today. For being so kind to my girls and agreeing to go dress shopping with Laurel."

Daphne smiles, and it's magnificent. Small creases form in the corner of her eyes, and her blue eyes shine just a little brighter as she walks back across the room, placing her palm on my forearm. It looks so small against my arm, her short nails painted a light lavender that compliments my olive undertones. "You don't ever have to thank me for that, Colin. I lost my mom when I was younger than they are now. I know how hard it is, how hurtful it can be to want to experience what everyone else around you is doing, while feeling left out because you don't have someone important by your side. If you haven't noticed, I kinda *really* like your kids, and that's saying a lot coming from a self-professed child hater."

I give a small chuckle as she continues. "They're great kids, Colin. You and your wife raised two wonderful girls. You should be proud."

"We did, and I am."

She gives me another smile, this one smaller than the last, before gently squeezing my forearm. "Sweet dreams, Colin."

I can't help but smile back, a genuine smile that I feel deep into my bones as I watch her walk away. "Sweet dreams, Daphne."

Turning off the lights throughout the house, I retreat to my bedroom, stripping out of my clothes and climbing between the sheets. And while I want nothing but those sweet dreams to come, I spend half the night Googling exactly what it means to be a little instead, thinking of Daphne with every eye-opening new discovery I find.

Five

DAPHNE

It's been a few weeks since Broken Sparrow reopened, and along with a glittery new floor—thank you very much for that brilliant idea—we also have appointment books overflowing with new and returning customers.

A gorgeous new reception area is the first thing customers see when they enter, one wall completely covered in artwork from local artists available for purchase. Six workstations are set up throughout the large, open space with an additional private room for customers looking for a more discrete experience. Top-of-the-line hydraulic tables can be used to bring a customer to a comfortable working height with the simple tap of a pedal, and our stock room has been completely transformed, making it easy to find supplies within seconds.

Standing in the middle of the space, I slowly spin in a circle, taking in the artists at work and the sounds of tattoo machines whirring over the low music piping through the room.

Raven, our super fucking cool receptionist, is busy helping

a few people with merchandise at the front of the store, flirting with every man and woman alike. I swear, that woman's charm has helped us to double our merchandise sales, and who the hell am I to judge if she uses a little sex appeal to do it?

I'm grateful that my books are usually slammed, sometimes months in advance. While I'm nowhere near the best, I've managed to build a bit of a following over the years for my fine-line black and gray artwork, and I'm still in awe on a daily basis that people trust me to permanently ink their deepest desires onto their flesh. Today, though, I can't help but let my gaze continually drift to the large clock that hangs in the shop, tapping my foot while waiting for Mina to finish up with her last customer of the day.

Just a few weeks ago, Mina and I teamed up to help Laurel shop for the perfect prom dress. After hours spent in more stores than I could count, two meltdowns where she almost wasn't the only one in tears, and one phone call to her dad to approve the three-hundred-dollar price tag, she picked out a stunning, long, dusty pink dress. Tight on the top with a low-cut sweetheart neckline, it's covered in sequins until it hits her waist where it flares out into a poofy, soft, tulle skirt. She decided not to show it to her dad until the day of prom, and there was no way in hell I was going to miss the reveal. Especially because she once again enlisted mine and Mina's help— this time for her hair and makeup.

I just don't know if I'm most excited to see her face when she comes out for the big reveal, or if I'm looking forward to seeing Colin as he takes in his firstborn in such an adult dress for the first time.

Damnit, these kids are making me go soft.

Finally, after what feels like hours but is, in reality, no more than forty-five minutes, Mina waves to her customer as he makes his way out of the shop. Practically tugging her along, I pull her toward the back door.

"Come on, come on, come on!"

She gives me a throaty little laugh. "What's the rush, Daph? We have a half hour till we have to meet Laurel, and it'll take us less than ten to get back to Colin's house."

Okay, so maybe I am pitter-pattering around like an excited little pup. I'm just nervous about this night going perfectly. "I'm just really anxious! This is a big night for Laurel...and for your brother."

We climb into my SUV and fasten our seatbelts in unison. "It's cute that you've taken an interest in the girls. I know they love spending time with you. And even if he doesn't say it, I think Colin kind of likes having you there, too."

I can't help the smile that spreads across my face. Within the first few days of living with Colin, the apprehension I felt about sharing a house with the often-stoic man melted away faster than a popsicle in the August sun. Seeing a different side of him, the one he reserves for when he is alone with his daughters, is refreshing, and when he honors me with one of those genuine smiles he saves for the rarest of occasions, it almost always takes my breath away.

"Those girls keep me on my toes, but it's really fun spending time with them. Colin's not so bad either. At the very least, he's easy on the eyes!"

Mina makes a gagging noise from the seat next to me, pretending to throw up. "That's just gross! Honestly, I thought by now you would have eaten him alive and spit him back out."

I giggle in response. "Want to know a secret?"

My best friend eyes me suspiciously. "I don't know—do I?"

"Sometimes, when I'm doing laundry, I'll *accidentally* leave a pair or two of my panties in the bottom of the washer for him to find."

"Daphne!" She feigns mock outrage, but her entire body shakes from laughter.

"The first time it happened was a mistake. But it riled him up and got such a fun reaction that now, I do it just to stir the pot."

It's not a total lie and was an accident that first time. My tiny little arms and equally short stature make it next to impossible to reach everything in the bottom of the washing machine. Most of the time, I resort to hoisting myself up so I can lean over the barrel and fish everything out from the bottom. Every time I do it, I swear I'm going to crack a rib. It's downright painful at times, so if a pair or two get stuck at the bottom of the machine and I don't feel like hurting my internal organs, I just leave them there for him to find.

"You really are too much. In the absolute best way."

We laugh and chat for the rest of the short drive. Despite working together almost daily, we don't have a lot of time between our clients and keeping Broken Sparrow running to devote to girl talk, so we find ways to fit it in whenever we can.

I've trusted Mina since the day I first met her over ten years ago. She knows every deep, dark secret that clouds my past, knows how I long to be cared for in the most basic of ways, and understands the desire I have to live in a world full of bright, colorful days and nights.

Mina has held my hair back while I've prayed to the porcelain Gods more times than I can count. She has gorged herself on greasy hangover breakfasts with me and opened her arms to me after the end of more than one failed relationship. Every step of the way, she's been there for me with compassion and empathy. I just know she'd make the best mother, and I hope she and Nico decide to take that chance in their relationship before I'm too old to enjoy being a cool aunt. Colin's girls have taught me that I'm not as afraid of children as I once thought myself to be, and I'd love to be by my bestie's side while she raises one of those little crotch goblins of her own.

Colin is in the living room when we walk into the house, Nico and Pauli as well. As always, I make a beeline for Pauli—Mama P as I like to call her—and give her a huge hug before giving Nico a much quicker side hug. Mina takes a seat on her husband's lap, wrapping her arms around his neck, and I excuse myself to change, yelling up the stairs to let Laurel know we're home and will come up to her room in a few minutes to get our makeover started.

As I'm pulling the oversized Broken Sparrow tee I wore to work over my head, a gentle knock sounds at my bedroom door. "Come in!"

With my back still to the door, I know it's Colin who has entered, and I lower the shirt I was trying to rid myself of. The man works magic on that damn door, never squeaking it when he pushes it open. I still haven't learned the trick, despite trying. One night, after everyone had gone to sleep, I even crept into the kitchen, finding a bottle of that weird spray butter the girls like for corn on the cob. I sprayed a few little squirts on the hinges, yet still, it squeaks every time I so much as look at the damn thing.

"Think we could work on remembering to check for all your delicates?" He holds out yet another pair of my panties, this time a black lace pair, dropping them into my outstretched hand.

Colin is starting to be almost nonchalant when it comes to my panty antics. I'm going to have to find a way to step up my game.

"Whoops." I give a little shrug, letting the stretched-out collar of the tee slide down and off my shoulder. My breath gets caught in my lungs when he reaches out to slide the fabric back into place. Sure, we've grown closer over the last few weeks, civil bordering on almost friends, but we're not the type of friends who adjust each other's clothes.

Are we?

His green eyes briefly shimmer, and I swear I can see the tiniest bit of mischief below the surface. "Somehow, *Little Girl*," Colin's voice is gruff as he steps even closer to me, "I don't think *whoops* is the whole truth."

He knows. I'm not sure how he found out, but somehow, he knows about me and he definitely knows I've been purposely leaving him my unmentionables that we mention quite a bit. Why else would he have called me little girl in an almost condescending tone?

If Colin thinks he can make me uncomfortable, he's got another thing coming.

Instead of stepping away, I close the distance even further. Hell, I've been well-behaved; I deserve to act up just a little. Tossing my panties to the floor like a petulant little child, I place my hand on his chest. It's hard beneath the fabric of his simple cotton t-shirt, and I itch to slide my fingers underneath the cotton, to bunch the fabric between my fingers and tug him to my lips. Slowly inching my hand down the solid plane, I look up at him through my long lashes. "There is one way to make sure it never happens again."

I expect him to immediately back away, to put space between us and remove my hand from his chest. He doesn't move, doesn't retreat. However, I do notice how tight his jaw becomes. Swear to God, the man could crack a molar with how hard he's gnashing his teeth together. "And what's that?"

Batting my lashes, I continue to inch my way down his chest, tempted by the feel of his muscles beneath the thin cotton of his shirt. "You could just do my laundry for me. Does the idea of my little girl panties mixing in with your big, manly clothes make you feel *dirty*? Or does it make you feel more like a *Daddy* than you already are?"

Just as my fingers are about to dance below the waistband of his pants, Colin's hand reaches out to snatch my hand away. I'm surprised he's allowed me to get even half as close to the promised land as he did.

His scruff is like sandpaper when he leans in until his cheek is barely touching mine, and his voice is equally as rough when he nearly growls in my ear, "Leave another pair of those panties in the washer, *Little Girl*, and not only will you not get them back, but I'll make sure you're punished for disobeying the rules I set in *my* house."

Colin wants to keep my panties? Wants to punish me?

There is no way. He must be trying to intimidate me.

Little does he know that those words do the absolute opposite.

Liquid heat spreads throughout my entire body before settling low in my belly. If this was anyone but Colin, I'd already be tackling them to the floor, ready to rub my greedy little body all over theirs. But despite these confusing as hell interactions we seem to keep having, I know if I so much as kiss him, he would shut down and run away.

He's across my room in a flash, almost through the door when I call out to him. "Hey, Colin?"

Hesitating for a second, he opts to look over his shoulder to meet my eyes instead of turning around to fully face me.

I shrug my shoulder so the collar of the tee falls down again. "What if you punishing me is exactly what I want from you?"

Then, with his eyes still on mine, I pull my shirt up and over my head, tossing it to the ground next to my panties. I watch as his pupils dilate, his nostrils flare, and his hands clench and unclench at his sides.. Frozen in place, his emerald-green eyes morph into two anthracite pools as they take in my bare chest.

My fingers slowly trail over my breasts, skimming across my nipples before moving to the button on the top of my denim shorts. "These are coming off next, *Daddy*, so unless you want to see what my panties look like when they're on my body, you'll want to at least turn around."

His torso snaps around, almost as if my words slapped him across the face, quietly letting himself out of my room, and I can't help the satisfied smirk that falls across my face when I'm once again alone.

Your move, Daddy.

Six

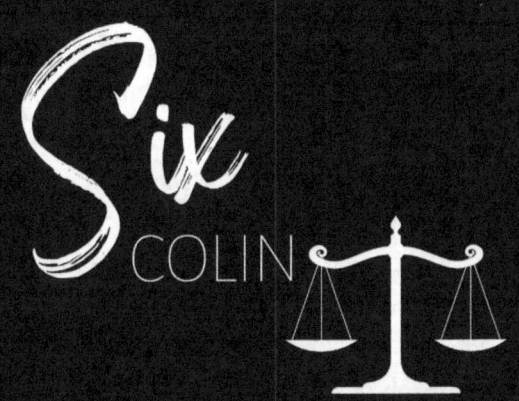

COLIN

WHAT. THE HELL. JUST HAPPENED?

One minute, I'm walking into Daphne's room, the room I used to share with my wife, to deliver yet another pair of her lost panties. The next, I'm staring at her as she lifts her shirt up and over her head, baring her chest to me like it's the most natural thing in the world.

And I couldn't look away.

Scratch that—I didn't *want* to look away.

The woman is beyond tiny in every sense of the word. I tower over her by leaps and bounds, and she can't weigh more than a hundred pounds soaking wet. Of course, she's stunning; there has never been any doubt in my mind of that, but when she peeled that oversized shirt over her head and tossed it on the ground, giving me unwritten permission to gaze at her body, at those little nipples that were peaked, and pink, and as delectable as raspberries picked fresh from the bush, I felt something that I hadn't felt in years.

Desire.

She's tight and taught, lithe and lean.

And suddenly, I find that I want to put my hands on every inch of that body.

That's how I came to be standing in my bathroom, willing my dick to deflate before I can even think of being in the same room with my family again. Over three years of celibacy and now is the time my body decides it wants to reenter the human race.

In the last six months of her life, before entering comfort care, Tabitha had undergone numerous treatments while trying her damnedest to fight the cancer ravaging her body. She lost her hair, her eyebrows, even her eyelashes. Some days, she couldn't find the strength to get out of bed, and often, she would tell me how even her skin hurt, making it painful for me to do something as simple as hold her hand.

Of course, the intimacy between us suffered. I spent more hours sitting in a recliner next to our bed than I did laying next to my own wife, and while I wanted nothing more than to climb into bed next to her and pull her into my body, I knew it would only cause her pain.

I read to her when she didn't have enough energy to keep her eyes open, helped her to drink small sips of water to keep her lips moist, and cleaned up more vomit than I ever did when either of my girls were babies. My needs were pushed far into the back of the closet, among the clothes you keep meaning to donate but never get around to actually doing so, replaced with the duty I had to my family.

It's a fate I wouldn't wish on my worst enemy—the cancer, not the role of a caregiver. Hell, I'd do that all over again for just one more minute with Tabitha.

That's why I'm so confused by the feelings coursing through my body right now.

I had my till-death-do-us-part, and like the greedy bastard

death is, he came and took my other half, leaving me alone to navigate life with half of my heart missing. You don't get the kind of love we had more than once in a lifetime, so what's the point of even trying—casual or not?

Rearranging myself in my pants, I take several long, deep breaths until I get myself under control. Whatever feelings I'm trying to sort through right now will have to wait. I have a daughter who is getting ready for her senior prom, and I need to be fully present for her.

I knock on Laurel's door, but it's Emily's face that pokes through the crack when it opens. "You're not allowed to see her until she's ready. Go back downstairs where you belong!"

"When did you get so sassy?"

She laughs, shutting the door in my face. Giggles seep out from under the door and follow me back down to the first floor.

Nico is the only one still in the living room when I return, a beer in one hand as he flips through a sketchbook with his other. "Daphne's or Philly's?"

While her friends and Nico always call my sister Mina, I grew up calling her Philly—short for her full name, Philomena. I'm fairly certain she hates the nickname, but it's a hard habit to break, and as her older brother, I'm entitled to get under her skin every now and again.

Instead of answering, he passes me the book. I open it cautiously, like something inside might reach out and bite me, thumbing through the thick pieces of off-white paper that are held together by a thick, spiral spine.

My sister was basically born with a pencil in hand, so I know instantly by looking that the work is not hers. However, what I see doesn't stun me any less.

Page after page of my girls, my house—hell, even my dog—fills the book. Beautiful pencil sketches of my daughters in the kitchen, a close up of Stella as she lounges in a puddle of sunshine on the back porch, even one of my mom that takes my breath away. In the sketch, the lines around her eyes are pronounced, each strand of hair drawn individually, and even the pores on her face are drawn with immaculate precision.

"Damn." I don't even realize I speak the word aloud until Nico responds.

"I have no idea what either of those women did to deserve the talent they got, but it's fucking impressive."

Not able to tear my eyes from the pages, I simply nod before I continue through the book, getting a raw and intimate look at my family through an outsider's eyes.

Daphne has managed to capture so much in such a short amount of time. She sees the beauty in my two young girls, the adventures my mother has lived that has given her such a zest for life, and even the graying fur that lines little Stella's aging snout.

I'm still mulling over the pictures, noticing that there is one glaringly obvious part of my life missing from this sketchbook, when Nico grabs my attention. "Hey, man. I don't know if Mina said anything to you, but the house should be ready next week, so you'll be able to get your peace and quiet back."

Closing the sketchbook, I place it gently on the table in front of me, aware of the precious contents within its pages. "Has she told Daphne yet?"

"Don't think so, figured you should know first."

My head clunks back against the couch, my eyes closing as I run a hand over the scruff on my cheeks and chin. It's a split-second decision, one I'm sure I'll regret, but my mouth starts moving before my brain can catch up. "Don't read too much into this. But maybe we don't tell her that it's ready yet..."

Even as the words leave my mouth, I know how ridiculous it sounds. I should take it back, but I don't. Instead, I just let the words hang heavy between us until I'm brave enough to open an eye to peer at my best friend.

An absolute shit-eating grin greets me. "Have the little panties she's been leaving around begun to crack through your tough shell?

"I said don't read into it, man."

Nico laughs, the sound echoing around the room. "The fuck I won't read into it. You guys shacking up, sharing a bed after the girls go to sleep at night? Damn, Col, I didn't know you had it in you, or rather, didn't think you'd ever get *it* again."

My mom and Emily enter the room, my daughter picking up the trail end of the conversation. "Get what, Dad?"

"Nothing, Em. Where's the rest of the glam squad?"

"On their way any second now!" I love how truly excited Emily is for her sister. Sure, at times, there is jealousy between the girls, like there is with any siblings, but helping her sister to get ready for a night that she doesn't even get to experience without jealousy makes my job as a parent even easier.

Not even a minute passes before Daphne and my sister come down the stairs.

My sister chirps, her excitement almost tangible. "She'll be down in less than two minutes for the grand reveal!"

Daphne skitters off to her bedroom, quickly returning with the colorful quilt from her bed. Grabbing the ottoman from the living room, she climbs on top of it, holding the quilt up to block the doorway while my sister does the same on the other side.

"Quite the production for a prom," Nico says.

Emily, in typical teenage fashion, rolls her eyes, giving her uncle a loud scoff. "It's not just a prom, it's her *senior* prom." She says it as if it should be obvious. And I guess, to her, it is. That rite of passage almost every high schooler looks forward to, the pinnacle benchmark of which to measure every slow dance against for the rest of their lives.

She may be the younger of the two, but she still is a fierce little warrior that is sometimes scarily wise for her age. An empath in every sense of the word, she truly feels the emotions of everyone around her, absorbing them into her own being. Sometimes, I worry she's growing up too fast, right in front of my eyes, but then she pulls a move like that little eyeroll and scoff combo, and she's back to the fourteen-year-old she should be.

The telltale click of heels on the hardwood floor signify the arrival of my eldest, Daphne's voice quickly filling the small living room once they stop. "Ladies and esteemed gentlemen, may we present to you, Miss Laurel Pappas!"

Both women drop the quilt hiding my daughter, and my eyes don't even fall on her for a full second before they're welling with tears. I stand and walk across the room, holding her at arm's length to take in every detail of this moment.

She'll always be my little girl, the sweet thing that I was afraid to hold when she was first born for fear of harming her delicate, little body. But today, standing in front of me isn't that little girl; it's a young woman who will be graduating soon. A young woman who will be going to college soon, who will be moving on from her life under her father's roof. Laurel makes it look so easy, so seamless to move on through her young life.

Is it time for me to begin to move on, too?

"You look absolutely stunning, Laurel. So much like your mom." My voice cracks when I speak, and I almost don't recognize the sound.

I hope it doesn't dampen her spirits for her night, but the resemblance is so uncanny, it is almost surreal. Laurel's copper hair is up in a sophisticated twist, a few strands outlining her round face. A tasteful smoky eye is painted across her lids, almost glittering when the light hits just right. Her lips have a dusty pink gloss coating them in a color that almost matches her beautiful, long dress. Each ear is adorned with tiny, silver hoops and when I see what is around her neck, I nearly lose any small ounce of composure I have remaining.

Hanging from a silver chain, a small charm sits against her skin with the imprint of her mother's fingerprint.

After her passing, I had one made for each of the girls. It wasn't a decision Tabitha and I had made together, but it felt like a special way for each of them to hold onto a piece of their mom, a way to have her with them for special occasions like weddings and at the birth of their future children. If I'm being honest with myself, I forgot about the charm necklaces and hadn't thought about them in quite some time. I certainly wasn't expecting to see it around her neck today.

Thankfully, I'm not the only one with tears in my eyes. My mom and sister are artfully sweeping at stray tears as they fall, trying not to bring attention to themselves. Daphne, never one to care what others think of her, lets the tears flow freely. Even Nico, all six foot plus of tattooed-covered muscle, has a far-off misty look in his eyes as he stands with an arm around my youngest, her little lower lip quivering as she watches the scene unfold.

We're all a mess in our own way, all trying to hold it together, until Laurel breaks the mood. "You're all going to ruin my makeup with these waterworks before we even get to take pictures!"

Quick to grab a tissue, Daphne is the first to step up to her, instructing her to look up at the ceiling as she lightly dabs the tears away from under Laurel's eyes in much the way a mother would. She takes care of my daughter, giving her a reassuring squeeze before stepping away.

Every move this woman makes slowly cracks my resolve,

slowly has me feeling like a man again for the first time in ages. She treats my girls like they are the most precious gemstones on Earth, and to me, they are. To me, her actions toward them speak more than any words she could speak aloud, and frankly, it's sexy as sin.

A small pang of guilt racks up my spine. I shouldn't be thinking about her that way. I shouldn't be quietly studying her as she continues to dote on my kids, shouldn't let my mind wander off to a dark corner where it is just the two of us and those damn underwear she leaves in the washing machine for me.

I shouldn't. I shouldn't. I shouldn't.

But I am.

"You're going to knock 'em all on their asses tonight, babe," she says to my daughter before turning to me with a saucy little smile. "Worth the price tag?"

The heart pumping somewhere deep within my chest, the same heart I believed to be irrevocably broken, begins to mend itself in just the smallest of ways. The first step of a marathon without any training before the race, but it's a step I'm more than happy to take.

I nod, giving her a small, unguarded smile of my own as I hold her eyes with mine, suddenly unable to look away.

"Worth every single cent."

Seven

DAPHNE

THE ABUNDANCE OF EMOTION SWIRLING AROUND THE house tonight has left me exhausted. Laurel left for her senior prom after no less than thirty-six-thousand-three-hundred-and-ninty-two pictures with her family (and another thousand or so with me), Emily has gone to be with her friend at a slumber party, and the rest of the adults have gone their separate ways—Pauli back to her condo while Mina and Nico returned to their home about a half hour from Johnson Creek.

It was truly a special moment, being able to witness the love that exudes from every pore of the Pappas family. Even more intimate was having a front-row seat for the emotional experience shared between Colin and his oldest daughter. It brought me to tears and touched something deep inside my own chest that had been buried beyond the rubble I haven't dared to fully climb out from under for years.

Watching him hug her close after taking in her form, seeing her as she melted into his strong body, watching as he doted over her and made her feel like the most precious young woman on Earth made me long for someone to treat me the same way. For someone to act as if I were some hidden piece of fine China that only gets used on special occasions as opposed to a disposable paper plate that becomes soggy with the least amount of use.

Shutting down when I get overly emotional has always been a survival tactic of mine, and while outsiders may think I wear my emotions on my sleeve, I do my damndest to try and hide them from people who don't know me well.

Today was especially challenging, helping Laurel to get ready, sliding the zipper up on the back of her beautiful, pink gown, and helping to secure her mother's fingerprint on the chain around her neck. I secretly loved that even with her aunt, grandmother, and sister in the room, she seemed to seek me out, almost if knowing that we share a bond created by the loss of a parent at a young age. It made me sad for her while also being equally sentimental for my mother, who I lost when I was only seven.

But now, I simply want to push it from my mind, fall into a comfortable head space that I so rarely get to enjoy since I moved into Colin's house, and fill my night with snacks, maybe a hot bubble bath, and soft, comfortable pajamas.

I expect Colin to retire to his home office, where he spends more hours than any one person should. We're rarely alone in the house, just he and I, but when we are, we seldom cross paths.

I'm about to pull a pair of flannel pajamas from my dresser, way too hot for the time of year but wanting to feel the soft fabric against my skin after my bath, when a knock sounds from my door. I'm slightly annoyed when I open the door, my plans for a quiet evening in my special space being postponed for whatever it is Colin needs to talk about. "Swear to God, it's only been a few hours since you were last in here! Christ, Colin, I haven't even done any more wash yet!"

He stands in my doorway, different from how he usually invites himself right into my room, into my space. He simply studies me for several seconds, his strong forearms crossed over his chest. It's making me squirm, equal parts uncomfortable and interested in what he wants. His face appears neutral, but there is something in his eyes that I can't quite make out. Uncertainty, maybe? Clearing his throat, he takes one, small step into my room, green eyes still trained on me. "Would you like to have dinner with me tonight?"

Well, that's certainly not a question I was expecting.

Colin must sense that it takes me by surprise. "Nothing fancy, maybe we walk down to Dina's Diner, get something to eat, then grab milkshakes for the walk back."

Shit, he had me at milkshake.

I wave my hand over my body, indicating the simple yoga pants and tank top that I have on. "Give me five to change, and I'm all yours."

It isn't meant to be flirty, still I don't miss the way Colin's nostrils flare in response. It's a small tell, but it is there, nonetheless.

We meet in the kitchen and leave through the front door, Colin holding the door open for me before locking the house behind us. Only a few blocks away, the diner has some of the best food I've ever tasted, along with the most delectable milkshakes known to man.

It's one of those places you expect to see on an episode of *Diners, Drive-Ins, and Dives*, a vintage-looking diner that still has plentiful counter seating along with several booths and tables. Small jukeboxes sit atop each booth, paper placemats advertising local businesses sit atop the tables, and you can smell the fryer oil the second you step foot in the door.

I'm not surprised when we arrive at the diner that Colin holds the door open for me. He has always been very much the gentleman, but it shocks the hell out of me when he leads me through the door with a hand on my lower back. My entire body thrums with energy, radiating out from his palm. It's gentle yet commanding at the same time, and it is a feeling I gladly accept.

We slide into opposite sides of a booth, our server quickly coming over to drop off menus and take our drink order. I recognize her as Steph, a friend of Mina's from high school. The pair reconnected when Mina moved home, and she was even a bridesmaid alongside me at her wedding to Nico. "Fancy seeing the two of you here together." She eyes us both suspiciously.

I blush, averting my gaze while Colin steers the conversation. "Yeah, Laurel has her senior prom tonight. Daphne did such a fantastic job helping her pick out her dress and helping her to get ready that I wanted to thank her."

"Geez, a senior already," she muses aloud. "Well, Hon, there is no better way to say thanks than with our food!" She shoots me a wink, letting us know she'll be back soon to take our orders.

Falling into silence, we both page through the overwhelmingly huge menu. It contains everything from breakfast dishes filled with bacon and pancakes to a full dinner menu, including homemade soups and sandwiches. That doesn't even take into account the over twenty types of homemade pie offered at the diner. It's what they're known for and what has put them on the map, even in such a small town like Johnson Creek.

Making a decision as simple as picking something off a menu should be easy, but when there are so many options, I often find myself overwhelmed. I know it sounds silly, but I worry I'll pick the wrong thing, worried that I won't pick what is the best of the best, and it can quickly send me spiraling into a place where I shut down, refusing to pick anything at all. I've missed more than one meal because of the same bubbling anxiety creeping up through my body right now.

Without knowing, Colin gives me an out when he lowers his menu and asks, "What are you going to get?"

I pull my bottom lip between my teeth, gently tugging on the flesh and releasing it when I notice Colin tracking the movement. "Actually, do you think you could order for me?"

He looks confused. "You want me to pick what you're going to eat?"

I nod while averting my gaze, somewhat embarrassed but knowing if I don't ask for it, that I'll end up watching him eat as I sit across from him with nothing but an empty place-setting in front of me.

This is just one of the facets of being a little that appealed to me when I first learned about the lifestyle. Having someone take care of me, to make decisions for me when it feels like they're too big to make on my own—it's a comforting feeling I can only liken to being wrapped in a fuzzy, plush blanket.

Colin must notice the fleeting panic that fills my face. His hands work to open his menu again, and he studies it for several long, silent moments. "Breakfast, lunch, or dinner?"

"Breakfast," I answer without hesitation, and wow...that was actually pretty easy, narrowing it down from what felt like hundreds of options to one of a handful of menu items.

Steph returns to our table to take our orders. Colin orders a steak sandwich for himself with onions, peppers, and cheese and a side of fries. When Steph turns her attention to me, he simply speaks again, commanding her attention much in the way he commands his own daughters. I imagine it is much the same way when he is in a courtroom full of people. Shit, I shouldn't find that sexy, but I wonder if he is the same way in the bedroom, too. "Daphne will have a number three breakfast special–extra bacon, chocolate chip pancakes, and scrambled eggs."

I can't help but beam up at him as Steph walks away. Never in a million years did I expect him to actually take the control I needed him to, even in something so simple as picking a meal for me. I know it doesn't mean anything, that it was him simply doing something I asked, but it still makes my heart soar.

"Thank you," I all but whisper.

He picks up his iced tea, taking long sips from it as the condensation cascades from the glass, dripping to the paper placement beneath it. "Thank you for today," he says as he returns the glass to the table.

"Nothing to thank me for. It was my absolute pleasure to be a part of Laurel's special day. Your girls—they're both amazing." I give him a squeeze across the table, quickly retreating when I notice the way he slightly straightens at my touch.

Somewhere in the diner, a tabletop jukebox starts, the sounds of music from long ago filling the space. It hangs between us, the lyrics swirling around while neither of us speak. We simply sit, looking into each other's eyes while we try to unravel the emotions the other is experiencing.

It's heavy and light at the same time, serious yet sweet, and I can't find it in me to tear my gaze away. I can't bring myself to stop looking into his tortured, green eyes, even as the tips of his fingers find their way back to the table, ever so gently caressing the back of my hand.

He does it just once before removing his hand, and damn it, I want him to do it again.

Hell, I want him to rip my clothes off and run those gentle fingers over every inch of my body, and I don't even care that we're in a diner full of people. Colin could take me here, could ask me to crawl across the floor to him in nothing but my birthday suit with a glass of the fancy whisky he likes to indulge in balanced on my ass, and I would gladly comply with his demands.

That little, almost minuscule touch and my body is alive.

Alive for Colin.

But it doesn't matter what my body wants.

It is not an issue that he is my best friend's brother or that he is almost ten years older than I am. It doesn't even phase me that he has kids and a dog—two things that I've never wanted.

I simply want him.

And at the same time my belly fills with butterflies, my heart breaks knowing that I'll never be able to truly have him. I've spent all this time trying to deny the feelings I've had for him, the growing urge in my very core to get closer to the extraordinary man who is such a damn good father that I wish I could call him my Daddy, too.

Colin can't be my Daddy, though. He can't even be a boyfriend or someone I casually date. I see the way he stares at the pictures that line the stairs. Family photos of tiny, little Emily and Laurel, him and Tabitha with their arms wrapped around each other, huge smiles on their faces while they were on family vacations or experiencing special occasions.

I see the way he rubs his fingers over the ring he still wears when he is stressed or lost in a memory. I see how, eighty-percent of the time, he looks through me instead of at me and I see how he is simply existing rather than living.

He is still so far lost in his own grief that I don't think he even wants to move on.

Setting two oversized plates of food in front of us, Steph is oblivious to the moment she has interrupted—the quiet, inti-mate moment of two people grappling with inner demons, too afraid to share their deepest fears with the other but trying desperately to find a way to build a life separate from pain and heartbreak.

If only he could understand that love doesn't have to be a once in a lifetime opportunity.

If only he would give me a chance to show him that it is okay to date again, to have fun again, to maybe even *love* again.

If only this was one of my favorite books where the hero always falls for the girl, a guaranteed happily ever after.

But it isn't something I can press. Hell, I know better than most that grief is a personal journey, it's a path that we each have to take on our own. It's something that can feel like it's resolved one day, only to punch you in the gut the next, and while it sometimes diminishes, it truly never goes away.

Colin picks up his knife, cutting his sandwich in half before taking a massive bite from the squishy roll. Second bite poised before his lips, I do the only thing I know that ever helps with my own grief.

I just hope he doesn't shut me down.

"Can I ask you something?"

He nods as he slowly chews. "What's up?"

"Will you tell me about Tabitha?"

Colin's body tenses for a fraction of a second before he melts to the booth. A beautiful smile breaks out over his face as if he's momentarily lost in some memory before he finally responds. "Absolutely."

We spend the next two hours talking, laughing at stories and memories of his wife, before each getting a milkshake and making our way home in comfortable silence.

Eight

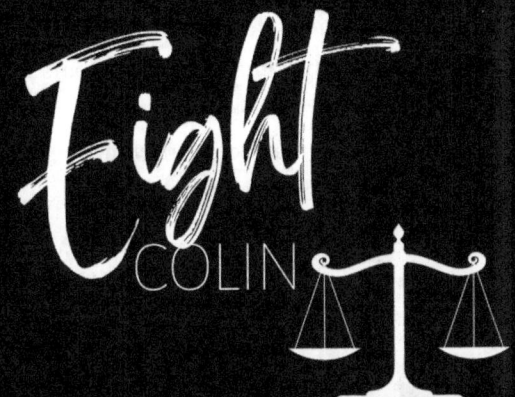

COLIN

My house on Bougainvillea Drive may look pristine from the outside. Perfectly manicured lawn, meticulously groomed flower beds, and not a centimeter of chipped paint. Take a few steps inside, however, and you'll quickly notice the inside is what many would consider well-lived-in.

Throw pillows often end up askew, pushed between the cushions and the back of the couch. The kid's belongings are scattered about, the few toys Stella still plays with at her age litter the floor, and there are usually at least a dozen half-empty water bottles in various places throughout the house.

But tonight, we've officially moved past well-lived-in, bypassed a huge mess, and landed straight in the middle of what I can only assume is a nuclear fallout zone.

Have kids, they say.

It'll be fun, they say.

Don't get me wrong, I wouldn't change it for the world. Well, maybe I'd ask them to be a little less messy, but that's beside the point.

Coming in through the side door to the house, I find myself in the kitchen. The usually clean island is littered with various bowls holding a multitude of what looks like pizza toppings. Cheese, pepperoni, mushrooms, bacon, peppers...you name it, it's there. Red sauce is dripping down the side of an open jar, pooling beneath it on the marble counter, and several personal-sized dough balls sit in a bowl with a damp towel being used as a makeshift lid.

I listen closely for a few seconds, noticing the silence in the house. For such a mess, it's just a little too quiet, and although my girls are now teens, I know that silence is the number one indicator that trouble is on the horizon when kids are involved.

Continuing deeper into the depths of the house, I find myself holding my breath, afraid of what I will find around the next corner. It's like I'm in a haunted house as I step quietly through the halls, waiting for something to jump out and grab me. Slowly, I peer around the wall to the living room, preparing myself for the worst.

I'm not sure if it is better or worse than I expected.

On one hand, there are plates with half-eaten pizzas scattered throughout the living room, a brownie with one bite taken out of the corner, and I can count seven empty cups and soda cans. Not one cushion is on the couch, the television screen is frozen on an advertisement for the latest Disney movie, and multiple slippers and books are strewn about.

But on the other hand?

The cushions from the couch have been piled high, a sheet from the bed in Daphne's room is perched across the pillows, creating a large tent in the middle of the room. Two air mattresses have been pushed together on the ground, blankets and sheets tangled in a mess on top. There is a soft glow cascading off a salt lamp that is plugged in on the built-in bookshelf, and barely audible music pours from a nearby phone.

Huddled under the blankets are my girls, each one flanking Daphne, who is equally as burritoed under her own blanket. At their feet, a quietly snoring Stella is curled up into a ball, her stuffed giraffe in her mouth.

It's a sight out of a movie—a sight that momentarily takes my breath away. My girls look relaxed. They look happy and content. A small smile curls Laurel's lips as she sleeps, and Emily clings tightly to a stuffed animal I've never seen before. Hell, even my dog looks more relaxed than she has been in months.

And then, there is Daphne.

I've said it before, and I'll say it again—there is no denying that the woman is beautiful. She's feisty and scrappy and a little rough around the edges, but I'm also learning she has a soft side, a more nurturing side than I ever thought possible. My girls quickly took to her when she moved in a few weeks ago, and while I initially had reservations about having her in my space, she has surprised me at every turn—offering to pick up the girls when I'm working late or cooking dinners for them when I'm beyond swamped.

I spend a minute taking in my surroundings, rubbing the ring on my finger as I let my eyes gaze between the three girls on the floor. Thinking back over the last few years, I feel slighted for my daughters. That living room sleepovers and junk food nights with their mom are a thing of the past, that they'll never have her for school functions and college visitations. My heart breaks when I remember they'll never have their mother for their own heartbreaks, that the woman who gave birth to them will never see them get married and have children of their own.

And like the selfish bastard I am, and as heartbroken as I am for my daughters, for the first time in over two and a half years, I allow myself to think that while I'll never have Tabitha back, that just *maybe* I could have a future where happiness isn't some strange illusion. That I won't have to wear a mask of contentment every day for the rest of my life. That maybe...just *maybe*...I could have a partner to share my life with once again.

When Daphne and I had dinner last weekend, she surprised me when she asked me to tell her about Tabitha. What surprised me even more is she genuinely seemed to want to know about my wife. She asked questions—so many questions. She laughed with me as I told her funny stories and even teared up when I recounted the hard-fought battle she waged against cancer before it took her life.

And while it felt odd at first, we ended up spending hours in that little booth, simply talking about the woman I love. There were times Daphne reached across the table, gently patting my hand with hers, nothing but a simple gesture to let me know she was there, and that it was okay to continue talking when I would get choked up. And after the first two times, I didn't even flinch when her skin connected with mine. It was refreshing to speak so openly with someone. Many days, Tabitha's name only brings apprehension. I'm afraid to talk about her in front of the girls for fear of triggering negative emotions, and I'm equally afraid to talk about her to my friends and family because I'm pretty sure they expect me to be further along my grief journey than I actually am.

But with Daphne, there wasn't any of that. She was simply there, reliving these moments alongside me as we ate and enjoyed our night.

My chest tightening even further, I force myself to push down the strange mixture of grief and silent anticipation threatening to spill over as I move deeper into the living room.

Quietly moving around the space, I tap the phone screen to turn off the music before dimming the light and turning the television off. I'm almost out of the room when I hear a soft voice call out to me.

Turning back toward the sleeping pile of girls cuddling together tightly, I see Daphne's sweet face staring back at me, a small smile on her full lips. She sweeps her gaze from the left to the right, taking in my sleeping angels before ever so carefully extracting herself from between them. Using caution, she steps over a still snoring Stella and quietly pads her way across the room until she's standing in front of me.

"I'm really sorry about the mess. Laurel was upset when I picked up the girls from school this afternoon. Something about fighting with a friend over a boy. You know how it goes."

She waves her hand in the air as if I know exactly how it goes before continuing in a softer voice than I've ever heard from the usually boisterous woman. "Anyway, I thought maybe a fun night would cheer her up, but I guess we all had a pretty rough sugar crash. I'll go to the kitchen now, and I'll make sure the living room gets cleaned up tomorrow."

Daphne makes to leave, and she's almost across the hall when I reach out, circling her delicate wrist with my hand. She stills, turning to look first at where our skin touches before trailing up to meet my eyes.

"Thank you." It's all I can manage to get out, my voice heavy with emotion. I want to say so much more at this moment, to thank her for being there for my daughters, for helping to feed them and care for them even when it cuts into her own time. I want to thank her for making me feel something again, even if it is something I can't or won't admit out loud to anyone, let alone myself, yet.

Because this woman makes me *feel*.

Maybe not from the first time I met her. Heck, not even when I most recently saw her at Mina and Nico's wedding. But over the last few weeks, since she's moved in, I've noticed her more and more. And it isn't just because she is in my space or leaving her panties for me to find. I've snuck glances at her when she comes in from a night out with my sister, watching as the soft curves of her feminine body move in whatever outlandish outfit she chose for the night. I find myself inhaling deeper, looking to get even a hint of her honeysuckle and vanilla scent.

And that first night with her panties, it's permanently etched in my brain.

When I entered her space that night, she stepped back, almost like she was afraid of me, afraid of what I was going to say. And maybe my tone was a little obtrusive, coming across more like when I scold my children than when I speak to another adult, but having that soft lace between my fingers did something to me down to my very core.

It made me feel like a man again. For the first time in God knows how long, my cock started to stiffen, and my body ached to touch soft skin. I wanted to inhale the scent of those panties, wanted to wrap them around myself and pump until I was drenching them in my cum. My fingers itched to reach out and tangle themselves in her long, flowing hair, to trail over her lips and fingertips..

I may have been an ass when I likened them to little girl panties, but the actual fact of the matter was, they were the sexiest little things I had ever laid eyes on.

Only after we had finished baking cookies and I retreated upstairs to my room for the night did I recognize that the face I saw when I thought of all those things was no longer my dead wife.

No, it was Daphne.

The very woman I have found myself thinking about over the last few weeks with an alarming increase speaks, pulling me away from my thoughts. "Colin, are you okay?"

I clear my throat, trying to remove the scratchy, sandy feeling that has taken up residence. "Yeah, just tired. Why don't you leave everything till morning. We can do it together."

She eyes me skeptically. "Are you sure? I really don't mind."

Glancing down, I realize I'm still holding her wrist, and her pulse increases under my fingers as we stand still as statues, just looking at each other. Never until this moment have I realized just how blue they are–a deep, dark blue that is so rich, it is almost navy, the same blue as the deepest oceans known to man. I want to swim in those twin blue pools, want to dive into the depths, and see where they lead. So different to my Tabitha's blue eyes, hers a lighter sky blue, but nonetheless, just as stunning.

Finally, after what feels like years have passed between us, I give her a nod. "I'm positive, Little Star. Go get some rest, and we'll take care of everything in the morning."

The small, sharp intake of her breath echoes between our bodies.

I have no idea what prompts the term of endearment to come tumbling from my lips, a term my father used frequently with my mother before he passed away. It isn't something I've ever used on my girls, not something I ever uttered to Tabitha. But right here in this moment, it's just so right.

In this moment, even as we part and make our ways to opposite sides of the house, her downstairs and me upstairs, it's all just right.

Having Daphne here is *right*.

Nine

DAPHNE

TODAY OFFICIALLY MARKS TWO MONTHS SINCE I'VE BEEN living with Colin and his daughters.

Eight weeks.

Fifty-six days.

One-thousand-three-hundred-forty-four hours.

It's gone by in the blink of an eye and as slow as maple syrup fresh from a cold tap at the same time.

As much as it feels like it is time to get a place of my own, to really get my life in Johnson Creek started, I get a hollow feeling in my chest whenever I think about actually following through.

Even moving in with Mina and Nico doesn't hold the same appeal that it once did, although at this point, who knows when my room at their house will be ready. It seems like every time I ask Mina about it, she has some excuse. Sometimes, I even wonder if she has changed her mind about having me move in with her.

But honestly, it's okay. There is something simply peaceful

living in the middle of the chaos that is Colin's house, as backward as that sounds.

I've even been able to fall into some semblance of little space when I'm around Laurel and Emily. Of course, they don't know about that side of me, and I'm sure as shit not about to broach that topic with them, but it's nice to be able to color when I want, snuggle on the couch with some of my stuffies while we watch movies together, and even spend time together in the kitchen baking cookies and brownies.

They're so innocent and pure, never judging me for doing something that could be perceived as babyish. It's beautiful and refreshing and makes me feel like I can be myself without judgment.

While many littles have a specific age or age range that they prefer to play in—with everything from using pacifiers up to enjoying activities designed for young teenagers—I've never really felt locked into a specific age. To me, being a little is simply allowing myself to feel and be small while knowing my inner child has never left my body, in embracing that inner child. It's in having a strong Daddy to nurture me, to help me make decisions, and to punish me when I'm acting like a brat.

I wish Colin would be the Daddy that would punish me when I'm being bratty.

My eyes trail him as he walks into the living room now where I'm sitting on the couch with the girls. It's late Sunday morning, a rainy day that canceled their plans of going swimming at their friends' house. Instead of still going to spend time with them, they chose to stay home with me.

When I tell you that my heart grew like the fucking Grinch when they asked if I had plans, if they could spend the day watching movies with me, I mean that it practically exploded from my chest with joy.

Two teenage girls choosing to spend time with me over

their friends. How awesome a feeling to feel wanted by them, to feel important in their lives.

Taking a seat in the recliner opposite the couch, Colin crosses one leg up over the other. If I angle myself in just the right way, I can almost see up his basketball shorts.

Not that I'm looking.

Kidding. I'm *totally* looking.

"You have plans today?" I'm not sure if he's asking me or the girls.

He arches a brow in my direction. Turning to my left and then to my right, I smile when I look at his girls. "You're looking at my plans."

"Don't you ladies think you should give Daphne a break?"

They aren't the only two who answer, all three of us creating a cacophony of stern "nopes" at the same time before we all burst into a fit of giggles.

God, I love these girls.

And that is equal parts terrifying and exciting—terrifying because I never saw myself as the type of woman who would become attached to someone's kids, never thought I'd actually look forward to spending time with them, nurturing them. Yet it's also exciting because there is a solid chance Emily and Laurel will be in my life for good now that I'm now in Johnson Creek. There's hope we'll be able to spend years bonding, sharing secrets, and creating memories.

Oh my God.

My stomach drops as soon as the thoughts enter my mind.

I basically just described the relationship that these girls should be experiencing with their mother, the love and connection that should be shared as they grow and mature, as they learn to navigate their lives. I could never fill the void their mother left behind. Hell, I wouldn't ever want them to think that I'm trying to replace her. Shit, have I been going about this the entire wrong way?

This entire time, I thought I was building a relationship with these girls and I truly thought it was beneficial for all of us. Could I be doing them more harm than good?

My skin is suddenly clammy, the little hairs on the back of my neck standing at attention, and I suddenly have the urge to get far, far away. Pushing from my seat, I'm halfway out of the room before I realize all their eyes are on me.

"I...uh...I'll be back in a few. I just remembered an important email I have to send." Even as the words leave my mouth, I know it's a lame excuse.

Making it to my bedroom door, I push it open, aware that it doesn't squeak today when it swings open. Grabbing my favorite stuffie from my bed, a giant, squishy octopus, I hold him close to my chest as I sink to the ground next to my bed. With my back propped up against the side of the bed, stuffie in hand, the tears I have been trying so hard to hold back pour out.

Even with my eyes closed, tears keep spilling. I can feel my body shaking as I let it all out, this sudden outburst of emotion coursing through my body with such ferocity.

"Daphne," Colin's voice calls in from the doorway. I turn toward the unexpected voice, and when he sees me on the far side of the floor, sitting against the bed, he enters without asking, quickly lowering himself to my side.

"Are you okay?"

I shake my head no, not wanting to lie.

"Tell me what's wrong." He doesn't ask me a question. Instead, he quietly demands it in a soft yet firm voice that has me blurting out my innermost feelings.

"I'm not trying to be their mom."

Confusion mars his beautiful face, and the sight is enough to have me continuing. "It's just, shit, Colin. I love them. I love them *so* much that it physically hurts my heart when I think about them being sad or scared or lonely. I never want them to feel those things, and it's a feeling that is so unexpected that it's scary."

More tears fall in big, fat drops that run down my cheeks before falling to my pajama shirt. "But then, I was thinking about how much I love them, about how much I want to build a future with them in my life, and it freaked me out. I don't want them to think I'm trying to replace their mom. Fuck, I mean, I don't even know why they would think that—it's not like I mean anything to you—but, I mean, I spend so much time with them, and I don't want them to get the wrong idea of me..."

I'm cut off by Colin's hand on my arm before he rasps, "Come here."

Pulling me from my spot on the floor, he helps me stand for the briefest of moments before he is sitting on my bed, pulling me onto his lap and wrapping his arms around me. I still from the unanticipated touch. "I'm too old to be sitting on the floor."

I attempt a giggle, but a stuffy-nosed huff is all that comes out.

One of his large, firm hands splays across my back. Gentle caresses run up and down my spine. It's intimate and reassuring, but there is nothing sexual in the gesture's nature. "First of all," he begins, his voice still somewhat lined with sleep, "you have been nothing short of amazing with both of those girls out there. They worship the ground you walk on, Daphne. And it isn't because you are trying to be their mother or take over her place in their lives; it's because of the very opposite. You give them the space to feel things and to explore all the emotions they have while never projecting your own onto them."

His hand stops moving, but he doesn't remove his hand from my back. "I've seen the way you tiptoe up to their rooms at night to say goodnight, the way you go out of your way to make sure they both feel included, even if it is something as silly as making cookies in the kitchen. I can only give them so much, but you...well, you give them everything they've been missing for the last two and a half years. You loving them—you'll never know what it means to me."

I cry harder, sobs wracking my body.

In a move hard to achieve, he pulls me even closer to his chest, my head resting against the hard muscle covered by only a thin layer of cotton. It's something a Daddy would do for his little girl, and it makes my stomach do a little flip, wishing so badly he could hold me like this for real.

"Second of all," one hand lightly trails through my hair, gently combing through the strands with deft fingers, "you mean something to me, Daphne. It's something I can't put a label on, something I don't know how to describe, but despite what I have led you to believe, you absolutely mean something to me, and it scares the ever-loving shit out of me."

Every ounce of air in my lungs is zapped from my body.

I turn as best I can atop his lap, needing to see his face, his eyes. Needing to know this isn't some cruel prank.

But when I turn around and see his eyes, there is nothing but honesty and vulnerability staring back at me. "Colin..." I whisper.

The hand from my hair snakes around to cup my cheek, his earnest, green eyes piercing me as his voice shakes. "Be patient with me, please. And while you're being patient with me, please don't *ever* stop loving my girls because they sure as hell love you, and they need you."

Nodding my head, I hold his gaze, afraid to look away for even a millisecond. "I'll never stop loving them, Colin. And I'll be here for you whenever you're ready—in whatever way you can give me."

It's the truth.

I'll wait for him as long as I have to, and when the time comes, I pray he can give himself to me fully because there is one thing I know for sure—without ever touching him, without ever kissing him or being intimate with him, Colin Pappas is the type of man I could fall in love with.

Hell, it might already be too late.

Ten
COLIN

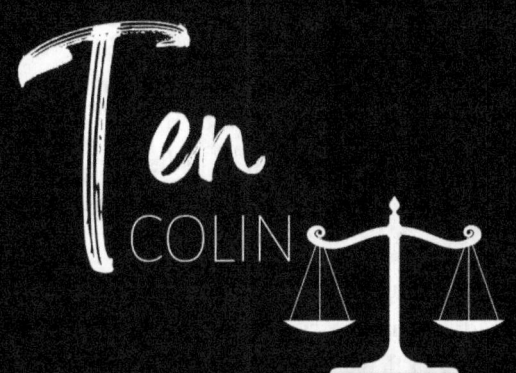

As seagulls soar overhead and the sun beats down on my now bronzed skin, I watch my girls as they run and jump, careening over small waves that crash along the shoreline.

Every year since Laurel was born, we've spent a few days each summer at the beach as a family. One of my favorite traditions, it doesn't matter how old the girls are, when we're here, they're not the teenagers they've grown to become; they're the two darling little daughters who learned to swim in these very waters. They are the two girls who tried saltwater taffy for the first time, laughing as they chewed and chewed and chewed and chewed before finally swallowing the sweet treats. The two greatest joys of my life who flew kites in the breeze after long days building sandcastles with their mother, grandfather, and grandmother.

And much like our Friday night dinners that have varied in numbers throughout the years, this year, our beach trip is different, too.

To my right, Nico sits reclined in a beach chair, a cold bottle of beer dangling from his hand. In front of us, my sister and Daphne lay on an oversized beach blanket, the corners being held down with various shoes and sand toys in an attempt to keep it from blowing down the beach.

Somewhere in the distance, music plays from a nearby group of beachgoers, the smell of grilled hot dogs wafts on the breeze, and all around us, the air is filled with the sounds of laughter and crashing waves.

I'm lighter than I have been in years as I close my eyes and tilt my head toward the sun. In a few weeks, my eldest will be at college, and I'll be down to just one daughter at home. It should terrify me, but I'm oddly calm as I think toward the future and what it has in store for my kids.

Daphne slams the book she has been reading shut, some sinister looking novel with a scantily clad woman wrapped up in the arms of what looks like a sea monster. Looking at my sister, she does a dramatic little stretch. "I'm bored as hell. I'll never understand how people can just sit at the beach for hours." She pushes herself to a standing position, stretching her arms up toward the blue sky before gently wiping some sand off her legs. "I'm going into the water to play with the girls. You coming?"

Following her best friend, both women walk toward the ocean, squealing in unison when the cool water hits their skin. They're quickly engulfed in the shallow water, jumping and laughing alongside Emily and Laurel as the waves hit their calves.

Nico reaches into the cooler between us, handing me a beer before taking another for himself. "Don't think I didn't see that."

I twist off the cap and take a long pull from the bottle, unfazed by the fact that it isn't even noon. "See what?"

"Come on, man. You can't bullshit a bullshitter. And I'm in real estate–I *know* bullshit." He downs half his bottle before continuing, jutting his chin to the ocean. "You're eating up that little, white bikini."

"If I was eating up that little, white bikini, don't you think I would have said something about it before you pointed it out? Maybe you're the one eating it up." I arch a brow in his direction, trying to play it off like he didn't just call me out. "Should I be worried there is trouble in paradise between you and my sister?"

My best friend's laugh is both boisterous and incredulous as he turns to face me in his too-small-for-his-large-frame beach chair. "You are so full of shit, Colin. All week, you've had your eyes on her. Tell me, brother, could you be starting to develop feelings for the tiny, reverse panty thief?"

Scratching the longer-than-usual scruff I've allowed to grow over my cheeks and chin, I release a long exhale as I look at Daphne in the water. The sun that has kissed her skin over the last few days has brought out a beautiful smattering of freckles across the bridge of her nose, and while I can't see them from this distance, knowing they are there is more than enough. White bikini or not, there is just something about the woman that drives me wild.

It's in her tattoos and small frame, in her raven hair and the stark contrast of her milky skin. It's in the tiny breasts that would easily get lost under the palms of my hands and the small gap that peeks from between her thighs when she wears the shortest of cut-off shorts.

But there is so much more than her looks, too.

It's why I asked her to be patient with me, why I'm seriously considering pursuing something with her despite the cold sweat that breaks out across the back of my neck every time I so much as think of getting closer to her.

"I am *so* fucked."

"Years of friendship and I don't think I've ever heard you drop the f-bomb. I'd say you certainly are fucked if she's got you talking like that."

I didn't realize that I had spoken the words out loud until he responded. "I'm sure you've heard me curse before."

My best friend full-on cackles. "So what does this mean? You going to go full-on Daddy Dom now?"

"One, fuck off." This earns me another laugh. "Two, I wouldn't even know where to begin with a woman like her, and three, I have no idea what a Daddy Dom even is. At forty-five, I've been with exactly one woman my entire life. I never expected to have to start over at this age."

Pulling the sunglasses from his face, he studies my profile as I continue to look ahead at the woman scampering through the waves. They lap gently at her thighs now, soaking the fabric that not so modestly covers her lower body. All the while she laughs, head thrown towards the sky as her hair cascades down around her back.

"I told her she meant something to me."

Letting out a low whistle, Nico opens the cooler again, this time opting for a bottle of water. "Does she? Actually mean something to you, I mean."

Without hesitation, I nod. "She loves my girls..."

I try to continue, but my friend cuts me off. "Christ, Colin, just once, don't think about the girls. What does she actually mean to *you?*"

Pushing everything aside that I feel for Daphne because of my daughters, I focus on myself, trying to not feel selfish for doing so. "She makes me feel things that I never thought I'd feel again. I look forward to seeing her before I go to work in the morning and actively seek her out when she gets home after a day at the shop. I find myself wanting to pull her into my arms when we're making dinner together, and I've had to stop myself from pulling her lips to mine more times than I can count."

As if it is the easiest thing in the world, Nico responds, "So, make a move. You already know she's attracted to you. It's just like riding a bike, my friend. Hop on that before someone else does because a woman like that doesn't stay unattached for long."

He doesn't give me time to reflect on his words before pushing up from his chair and grabbing a nearby football. Halfway between the chairs and the ocean, Nico turns and looks back at me where I am still sitting in my chair. "Come on, old man. Time to take off the training wheels!"

With a confident, easy swagger that I'll never possess, he reaches the water in a few more steps, sweeping my sister up into a hug before tossing the ball to Emily. She easily catches it, tossing it to her sister.

"Colin!" Daphne's voice reaches me over the sound of the waves as she calls out to me. "Get your ass in the water before I make you regret inviting me along on this trip!"

I drain the rest of my beer, already warm from the summer sun, before pushing up from my chair to the sound of cheers. Rolling my eyes and entering the water with a grin,, I quickly catch the ball spiraling toward my face before launching it back to Nico.

The two of us might be in our forties, but we've still got it.

The six of us fall into an easy game, throwing and catching the ball while jumping over waves. Every so often, one of my girls tries—and fails—to tackle their uncle or myself. Several throws go long, veering off into the ocean as we all scurry to reclaim it before it's swept out to sea.

As I chase after one such long ball, laughing when a wave blindsides me, Daphne darts in front of me, unsuccessfully trying to grab the football. While I haven't been able to hold something over my head and out of reach of my kids for a few years, Daphne is so adorably compact that when I hold the ball high over my head, she doesn't stand a chance. Still, it doesn't stop her from jumping up and down, repeatedly trying to knock it from my grasp.

"Keep that up, and you're going to fall right out of that little thing you call a suit."

Her eyes flash with defiance as she continues to jump. "Maybe that's exactly what I'm counting on."

I quickly glance behind her, making sure no-one can hear us. On her next jump, she almost gets her fingertips on the ball, and I stretch my body even more, keeping it out of her hands.

Daphne's eyes widen as they trail down my torso, and I follow her gaze until it stops where my board shorts have shifted down—lower than is decent for any public beach—showing the small, rose tattoo on my very lower hip. It was something I did on a whim at nineteen, something I don't spend time thinking about, but something she has teased me relentlessly about since she learned I had a hidden tattoo over two years ago.

"A rose?! On your hip?!" she squeals, all thoughts of trying to capture the football quickly forgotten.

"Don't you say a thing," I warn her, adding another silent warning in my stare.

Those beautiful, blue eyes flare again before she opens her mouth.

Before she can say anything, I yell to Nico, throwing the ball back to where he stands with my sister and daughters. Then, tugging up my swimsuit, I turn my words back to Daphne. "You want to reveal my secrets? I don't think so, Little Girl."

I pick her up effortlessly, depositing her over my shoulder as I stalk into the deeper water. She shrieks before laughing, her arms reaching around my waist as she hangs upside-down. "What are you doing? Put me down!"

Laughing in response, a guttural laugh that reverberates through my body, I don't stop until I'm deep enough that the water will certainly be over her head. All the while, she contorts her body, climbing up me to keep her head above the water. "You want me to put you down?"

"Yes!"

She squeals in delight when I toss her in the water but quickly realizes her mistake when she tries to stand. "Not fair!" She flails for a few seconds before her lithe legs find my torso through the water, and she wraps them around me tightly. Her arms find purchase around my neck, and she hangs onto me as if she would be the next thing swept out to sea without me under her body.

It feels...good.

But also dangerous.

One hand drops under the water and dips below the waistband of my board shorts, her fingertips trailing over the spot where the rudimentary rose is etched on my skin. "You're simply full of surprises, aren't you?"

I can't speak, can't find my voice with this woman's body pressed against mine, small breasts barely covered by flimsy fabric molded against my bare chest, her fingers continuing to travel over my exposed skin. Of course, she senses my hesitation, speaking while I struggle to form a coherent thought. "Like when you call me Little Girl," she presses herself closer to me, "that's a surprise that I really, *really* like."

My arms reach around her to steady our bodies right before a wave pounds against us, nearly knocking us over. I start to walk us back to the shallows with slow, measured steps as my feet find purchase on the shifting sand under them. Somewhere in front of us, I swear I hear my best friend as he says, "He is so fucked."

Keenly aware of the eyes on us and open mouths staring in our direction, I quickly drop my forehead to Daphne's for a fraction of a second before I can growl out the words plaguing my thoughts. "Little Girl, what are you doing to me?"

Just like riding a bike, my ass.

Eleven

DAPHNE

SILENCE HAS FALLEN OVER THE HOUSE RECENTLY, AND I hate it.

Ever since Laurel left for college a few weeks ago, Colin has been even more stoic than normal, Emily has barely had the desire to do much of anything, and even old lady Stella has been moping around the house in an almost constant state of melancholy.

Of course, I miss her too, going as far as to text her every few days to make sure she is okay and sending her a care package full of her favorite snacks and a couple of low-spice romance novels she asked to borrow. But I know she's only a few hours away and will be back often to visit, which makes me feel a little less sad when I think about her now empty closet upstairs.

It's not a secret to Colin and his girls that I lost my mom when I was only seven, but it is a secret to most—them included —that on the night I lost my mom, I also lost my dad.

Even almost thirty years later, I can recall the details of that night with near-perfect clarity. The way my dad screamed at my mom as smoke plumed in the kitchen from the charred dinner that was in the oven, the stench that hung heavy in the air from the way he chain-smoked in his recliner each night, the way my mom's terrified eyes found mine across the room before she simply yelled at me to run.

I'm not sure if it was that I was just noticing things more as I aged or that the abuse had gotten worse over the years. My mom was my protector, always keeping me out of harm's way, often at her own expense. Knowing now what I do about their tumultuous relationship, I think she knew that this night was the last time she would face his wrath, that it was the last time she would be there to protect me and that in her final moments she would do whatever she could to make sure I was safe.

I listened to her simple urging to run, my bare feet carrying me out the front door and into the cold December night. The neighborhood was decorated for Christmas, colorful lights lining every house but ours. Running until I reached my neighbors, an older couple with no children of their own, I pounded my little fists on their door, shaking from a combination of fear and the icy chill in the air. As the husband opened the front door, peering down at me as I stood in my pajamas on their doorstep, a shot rang into the night air, and he ushered me into his house and into his wife's arms before calling the police. They arrived just minutes later, but it was already too late—my beautiful mother was gone, and my father sat silently in his recliner, a cigarette burning between his lips, before turning the gun on himself.

Not just that night but also the abuse my mother received at the hands of my father leading up to that night, shaped me into the person I am today. It's why every single spot on my body can be freezing and I won't care, but the second that cold- ness spreads to my feet, I have to grab multiple pairs of fuzzy socks and slippers to combat the feeling. It's why I've never dated a smoker, why I have a rule to not indulge in more than a few glasses of alcohol, and why I always worry—even now—that the people I get close to will always end up leaving me, will be taken from me.

When you experience a tragic loss—whether it be the loss of a parent at the hands of the other or the loss of a wife and mother from cancer—you start to view every subsequent loss differently. Even something as simple as a daughter leaving for college can trigger those memories of grief and loss, and while you know on a conscious level that the person will return, that they're not gone forever, on a subconscious level, you worry that you'll never see them again, that you'll lose them, too. Hell, I even felt that way when Mina bested me, coming to Johnson Creek two years ago.

Like I said, I get it better than most.

But while I get it, I also know it's unhealthy as fuck to wallow in those unsubstantiated feelings and that it's a slippery slope that can quickly lead back into unhealthy coping patterns and deep depression.

Trust me, it took years of extensive therapy to get to a point where I could understand my complicated emotions without falling into long nights of heavy drinking to escape how I was feeling.

So yeah, I'm going to allow Colin and Emily to have their feelings, but I'm not going to let them wallow any longer.

We're going to have some fun, damnit!

Standing at the bottom of the steep steps that lead to the second floor, I holler up to the two hermits. "Colin, Emily!"

One by one, they exit their rooms, coming to stand side-by-side at the top of the staircase like two tin soldiers standing in perfect formation.

"You guys have twenty minutes. Get dressed. We're going out."

Two pairs of eyes stare back at me, but I don't relent. I pop out my hip, placing my hand on it for extra emphasis before looking up at them. "You heard me—get ready!"

Without waiting for a response, I turn and walk back to my room, where I throw on shorts and a tank top before brushing my teeth and throwing my hair into a messy bun on the top of my head. It isn't that I'm opposed to wearing my hair down, but that damn messy bun gives me the illusion of being a few inches taller, and I'll take any added height I can get, even if it comes in the form of a pom-pom on the top of my head that sways a little every time I take a step.

Exactly twenty-three minutes later—yeah, I timed them— we're in my car headed to the giant arcade that just opened in the next town over.. An enormous smile spreads across my face as Emily continually tries to guess where we're going and even Colin throws a guess or two of his own into the mix.

After parking and entering the building, I walk to the counter and buy three all-you-can-play passes. Handing one each to Colin and Emily, I hold on to the third. "Well, where are we starting?"

"Skee-Ball!" Emily says as she clutches her card, taking off in the direction of the row of machines lined up against the back wall of the building. It's a rare moment where I get to see her acting as a true fourteen-year-old as opposed to the girl who had to grow up sooner than expected when her mom passed.

Colin and I are closely behind, albeit at a much slower speed. The sounds of pinball machines, air hockey tables, and classic video games echo around the building, making it hard to hear the pop music being pumped into the arcade. "I didn't even know this place existed."

Shrugging, I reply, "Maybe you need to get in touch with your inner little a bit more."

Momentarily, I pause, aware it is the first time I have so blatantly acknowledged that side of myself in front of Colin. My cheeks heat in embarrassment, and suddenly I wish I hadn't left my sunglasses in the car so that I could slide the oversized frames over my face in an attempt to hide.

He takes a few steps before realizing I'm no longer at his side and quickly returns to me. "What's wrong?"

There is actual concern in his question, and it shouldn't surprise me. After all, he is a fantastic father and knows how to read the emotions of his girls with almost expert precision. After a few months of living under the same roof, it would only be fair to assume he has started to learn how to read mine too.

Instead of verbally giving a response, I give my head a quick little shake, the bun atop my head slipping to one side..

A large hand gently presses against my lower back, and I can't help but suck in a breath at his firm touch. How utterly safe and cherished I feel with such a small gesture despite the embarrassment that lingers. Ushering me in the direction of Emily and our awaiting Skee-Ball game, Colin speaks so softly that I almost miss his words over the din of the arcade. "You don't have to hide who you are from me, Little Star."

I'm taken aback at his gentle words and tender touch. Confused, but unwilling to break the contact.

We spend the remainder of the morning and well into the afternoon playing games, joking, and laughing together. I whip Colin's ass at air hockey, he schools me at a basketball simulator, and Emily beats both of us at enough rounds of Dance Dance Revolution to put us to shame.

More than once, I catch Colin out of the corner of my eye, and every time I do, he seems to be carefully studying me. When I turn my head toward him, he doesn't turn away.

Instead, he looks at me with kind eyes and a small smile, which I gladly return. Surprising me even further, after Emily runs into a friend from school and scurries off to play a few games with the girl, he pulls me into a hug. It's quick, yet it takes my breath away when he gruffly says, "Thank you for today. I think we all needed it."

Our little game-playing trio racks up more tickets than we know what to do with and while Emily trades in enough to score a new crafting kit, phone case, and some candy, I excuse myself to use the bathroom before we leave to drive back to Johnson Creek.

Father and daughter are already in my car when I open the driver's side door to crawl behind the wheel. Sliding the key into the ignition and pulling my seatbelt over my chest, I finally look at the steering wheel and gasp at the little stuffed toy perched atop the wheel. The top, a round and chubby little cat, tapers down into a colorful mermaid tail with scales in pastel pinks, purples, and blues. There are six little shells over where each of the cat's six nipples would be and long, pink hair that cascades down the back of the toy. It's frilly and glittery and absolutely perfect.

My eyes scan the rearview mirror where I find Emily already glued to her phone before my gaze turns to the man sitting next to me.

"No more hiding," he says with a small wink. "Thanks again for a fun day."

Placing my right hand on his left thigh, I give him a gentle squeeze before putting my new favorite stuffie on my lap and shifting the car into drive.

When we arrive home, Emily and I settle onto the floor in the living room, where we tear into her new craft kit, my little mermaid kitty sitting dutifully by to watch as we weave colorful friendship bracelets.

Colin orders dinner from Dina's Diner and offers to walk down to pick it up. After he leaves, Emily turns to me from her spot on the floor, holding out her completed bracelet. "I know it must be weird to hang out with a kid like me all the time, but I really am happy that you're in my life, Daphne. Would you wear my friendship bracelet?"

Tears well up in my eyes as one hand comes up to rest over my chest. "I'd be absolutely honored, Emily. And it's never weird to hang out with a kid like you. You're one of my favorite people in the world, and besides, you're not really a kid, you're a young woman."

I give her a little wink as she beams at me, tying the colorful corded bracelet loosely around my wrist. I can't help but return the sentiment, smiling brightly right back at her as I tie my own creation around her wrist. "I'm really happy you're in my life, Emily." Hoping she knows how true my words are, I pull her into a huge hug.

"Me too!" she responds with more enthusiasm than I've seen from her over the last few weeks, and I can't help but feel like our little arcade outing was just what we all needed to get back on track.

We settle back into a quiet routine, each working on our own projects until she breaks the silence. "Can I ask you a question?"

"Of course, babe. You can ask me anything." I supply the answer without taking my eyes off the small, ceramic unicorn I'm now painting.

"Are you in love with my dad?"

Stunned by her question, I still the brush I'm holding over the unicorn and turn my full attention to my little bestie. "I care a great deal for your dad. He's a fantastic man and has become a friend to me." Thankfully, she doesn't quite catch on to my side-step of her actual question.

Emily seems to think for a minute, not returning her attention to her own project. "I...I think he wants to love you, but that he is afraid. You know, like he is afraid that if he loves you, he'll forget about mom."

"How did you get to be so smart?" I toss my brush onto the cardboard I have been using under my painting and pull her into my lap.

She doesn't answer my question verbally. Instead, she loops her arms around my neck. At fourteen, Emily is already taller than me, but I still feel protective of her in this moment. Almost...maternal. "I don't think he will ever forget my mom. I know I won't. But still, I want him to be happy again. He used to laugh and smile a lot more before she died. And it's started to happen again—ever since you moved in."

"So, what do you think I should do?" I ask, not at a loss of the fact that I just asked the fourteen-year-old daughter of the man I'm swooning over to help me with ideas on how to get him to see me as something *more*.

"Help him not be afraid," she replies almost instantly. Her voice holds so much conviction, making her sound so sure of herself. "Help my dad see that he can love you and still love my mom, too."

I can't help but press a kiss to the top of her head. "I love you, kiddo."

"I love you too."

Returning with several large bags of food, Colin pops his head into the living room, shaking his head as he looks down at our mess before asking Emily to set the table for dinner. She skitters off to the kitchen after a quick, "Yes, dad," and I can't help but be a little playful after the truly enjoyable day we all shared, as well as the tender moment I had with Emily mere moments ago.

I grab my stuffy, holding it close to my chest and push up to my knees. Doing my best to bat my lashes and pout my lips at Colin, I look right into his gorgeous, green eyes and do my best to purr out in a seductive voice, "Yes, Daddy."

Hey, Emily asked me to help make her dad smile and laugh more, and he said I didn't have to hide from him anymore.

I'm just seeing if he actually means it.

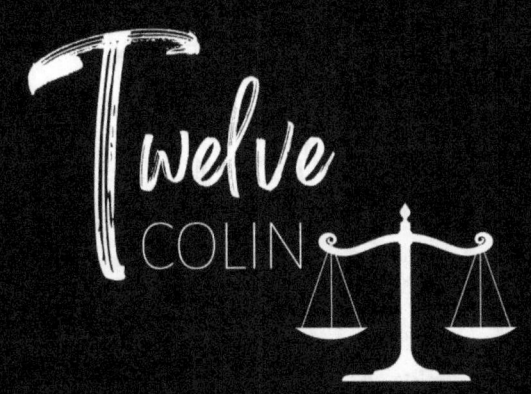

Twelve
COLIN

I ALMOST KISSED MY SISTER'S BEST FRIEND.

What the fuck is wrong with me?

And when did I start saying fuck so frequently?

All night, I tossed and turned in bed. I couldn't get the image of Daphne on her knees out of my head, those big blue eyes staring up at me from under heavy, black lashes. It didn't matter that she was fully clothed or that she was on the ground with my daughter playing with Emily's new craft kit she got with arcade tickets. When she pushed to her knees and locked eyes with me before playfully murmuring, "Yes, Daddy," I almost came in my pants right there in the living room.

I know she was only joking, following in the footsteps of my kid who gave a quick "Yes, Dad" when asked to set the table for dinner, but I couldn't help myself.

The second Emily was out of the room, I hauled Daphne to her feet, walking her backward until she was flush against the wall. A hand on either side of her head, I leaned into her until our lips were nearly brushing, breath mingling in the space between us, and only a nanosecond away from kissing her... until the spell was broken when my child started screaming about dog crap on the kitchen floor.

Retreating to the kitchen to clean up the mess, we then spent the rest of the night avoiding each other, never fully able to make eye contact with one another. Still, it didn't stop me from thinking about her all night long until I couldn't take it anymore. Until my hand snaked down the front of my briefs and wrapped around my cock when I was alone in bed. Until I found myself uttering her name as I made a mess all over my stomach.

The regret filtered in almost immediately, shame coursing through my body when I turned over in bed to see the wedding picture of me and Tabitha looking back at me from my nightstand—our young, smiling faces filled with promises of forever. It made me sick and I found myself over the toilet, vowing never to eat spaghetti from the diner again.

Thankfully, court was canceled this morning, so after sending Emily to school, I was able to fall back into a restless sleep. Of course, I found myself dreaming of the raven-haired beauty taking up residence in my house, which only unsettled me more.

I push a few papers around on the desk in my home office where I've been sitting for at least two hours before I rub my temples. Glancing at the clock and in desperate need of more caffeine, I quietly open the door and walk the short distance to the kitchen.

Daphne is standing naked in the kitchen, and she gasps when I walk into the room. Her feet turn into concrete, not allowing her to move from the spot. Instinctually, one hand comes up to shield her tiny breasts, the other cupping herself between her legs, hiding herself away from my eyes the best she can.

The late morning sunlight streams in through a stained-glass window placed over the kitchen door. It was a concession on my part when Tabitha and I purchased the house, her wanting to bring a bit of old-world charm to the place, me wanting to modernize what little had not already been transformed. We fought about that window for weeks, but in the end, Tabitha won and the window stayed. She always won, and she knew it. I was so tightly wrapped around her little finger, wanting nothing more than to give her the world. Until that same cruel world decided to take her from me.

And now, through that very window my late wife loved and fought for with such passion, the gentle sunbeams cascade over another's body, painting a picture on her skin more colorful than all her tattoos combined. Daphne looks almost ethereal as she stands there with her arms draped over her small frame. Her hair is damp, hanging over her shoulders, the tips of her hair almost brushing her nipples. Chaotic blue eyes dart to mine before flitting away, focusing on anything in the kitchen but me.

I can't help but reach for the ring on my finger, casually rubbing at the metal of the band, memories of Tabitha assaulting me while I stare straight ahead at another woman.

My own eyes stay fixed on her, studying every slight curve of her body. I notice both of our breathing has become labored. I should turn around and walk out of this kitchen. Hell, I should walk out the door behind me and not come back until I know she is gone for good. I should feel guilty for openly staring at her, guilty for the thoughts creeping in that make it feel like I'm cheating on my dead wife.

But I don't.

It makes me feel sick and relieved at the same time. Maybe I'm trying to rationalize the feelings growing within, the growing attraction I feel for Daphne, but deep down, with the sunlight framing the little pixie in front of me, I almost feel like this is Tabitha giving me a message.

Telling me that I should move forward with my life.

Telling me that I *need* to move forward.

Daphne breaks the silence, her voice uncharacteristically quiet and reserved when she speaks. "I...I'm sorry. I thought everyone had left for the day. I called out, but no-one answered."

I stride toward her, closing the distance between us. She tilts her chin up as I come to rest in front of her, the arm cradling her breasts close enough to my chest to brush against the fabric of my shirt with each inhalation. Without thinking, my large fingers trail across her chest. From one shoulder to the other, I drag them slowly across her skin, watching as goose-bumps erupt in their wake. Her skin is smooth beneath my touch, a hundred silk scarves that I want to run between my fingers and along my skin. It's supple and lush, still pale and creamy despite the fall sun we've been having with just the barest hint of freckles.

She sucks in a breath as I run my hand over her arm, lightly circling her wrist before pulling her hand away from her body, exposing her bare chest to my hungry gaze. Her arm drops to her side, nipples pebbling into perfect little pink points as the morning air licks against her bare skin.

Bending at the waist so I'm almost eye level with Daphne, I brush her hair over one shoulder before placing a kiss behind her ear over a tattoo of a beetle. Moving to her shoulder, I kiss the mandala that stretches over the surface before trailing kisses down her arm, one for each of the colorful designs that decorate her body. Repeating the process on the other arm, she lets out a small gasp when I kiss the inner crease of her elbow, where a small collection of colorful gemstones are etched on her flesh.

Without waiting for another response from her body, I drop

to my knees on the kitchen floor as her hand moves from where she was previously shielding me. My hands come to find purchase on her hips, and I get lost in the way my large hands look spread around her petite body. I feel powerful, and even more so, protective of her.

I bring my lips to the apex of one hip bone, kissing the sprigs of wildflowers blooming across her skin before moving to the other hip, trailing my nose over her smooth skin as I go, inhaling her blossoming arousal. Pausing to read what is inscribed on the two large candy hearts, I chuckle when one reads *Good Girl* while the second reads *Choke Me Daddy*.

Daphne does as instructed when I motion for her to turn around, her feet skittering on the cool floor in quick succession. I reach up and trail one finger down the length of her spine, over the phases of the moon, before making my way back to the top of her neck, kissing from right above her tailbone, up...up... up until I lay one final kiss at the base of her neck.

Instead of turning her back around to face me, I take my time walking from behind her until I'm standing in front of her again, my cock noticeably straining against the fabric of my pants. Daphne's eyes dart away from mine, but with one finger under her chin, I redirect her gaze back.

Needing to feel more of her, I tug her forward by one arm until her naked body is flush against my clothed form. My hips roll forward, grinding against her with need in a movement she reciprocates, a needy little mewl spilling from her otherwise silent lips.

It takes a lot to make Daphne shut up, and I smirk to myself, knowing that I may have stumbled upon the exact way to do just that.

One hand skates up her back and around the base of her neck before it comes to tangle in her hair. With a gentle tug, I pull her hair until she is looking up at me through wide, blue eyes. A cocktail of emotion swirls in those twin blue pools—a tentative curiosity, a hurricane of desire, and something else I can't pinpoint at the moment. But it's something I plan on uncovering.

"You're fucking gorgeous."

A huge grin breaks out across her face, her eyes igniting to the point where I can finally see that last emotion—defiance.

"Colin Pappas," she coos, "did you just curse?"

My fist tightens in her hair, and a small whimper passes into the space between us. "Shut up, Little Girl."

I smash my lips to hers, crushing her with the force of nearly three years of need and frustration. Almost three years of the desire for the simplest form of human contact, of the smooth skin of a woman beneath my fingers, and the even more delicate skin of her lips against mine. Almost three years of thinking I would never have it again.

And now, in my kitchen with my sister's best friend, I have it all.

Her lips taste like butterscotch and sin, a tempting combination that could easily become my new favorite flavor.

My entire body is on fire as her hands fist in my shirt, bunching the fabric to tug me even closer to her body.. I lick against the seam of her lips, and she opens for me. Our tongues tangling together, I explore her body with my free hand, the other directing our kiss as I tilt her head this way and that.

Daphne pulls away, her naked chest heaving as she tries to suck in the air around us. She reaches up to touch my face, the pad of her thumb skating across my bottom lip as she bites at her own, worrying the flesh between her teeth. "Take me to bed, Colin."

She's breathy and seductive, a little siren sent out to sea to lure me back to living a life in color when I felt destined to stay in the boring world of black and gray. Her lithe body and audacious attitude, determined to break me.

And I might just let her.

Easily lifting her into my arms, Daphne wraps her legs around my waist and her arms around my neck. Nuzzling into my neck, she licks and bites, leaving little kisses on my skin as I carry her to her room.

Thirteen
DAPHNE

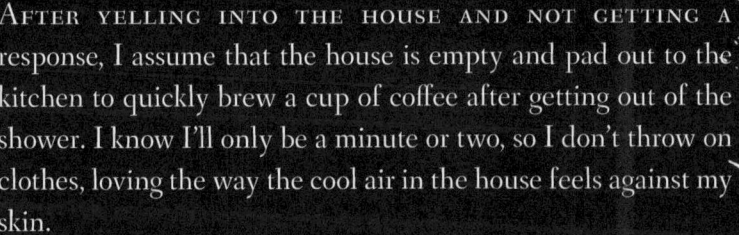

AFTER YELLING INTO THE HOUSE AND NOT GETTING A response, I assume that the house is empty and pad out to the kitchen to quickly brew a cup of coffee after getting out of the shower. I know I'll only be a minute or two, so I don't throw on clothes, loving the way the cool air in the house feels against my skin.

But you know what they say about assuming...

His energy permeates the kitchen a split second before he strolls in, yet I can't help but gasp when my eyes collide with his. My hands move on their own accord, one resting against my poor excuse of a chest while the other cups my pussy. I've wanted this for years, wanted him to see me in my absolute barest form, yet I can't help but shield myself as if silently protecting my body.

Although my hands shield much of his view, his eyes rove over my body like he can see every bit, and while his breathing has picked up, his face stays impassive, not showing an inkling of his innermost thoughts.

I take this opportunity to make my own silent perusal of his body, loving everything I see. Colin wears faded flannel pajama pants while a white thermal shirt clings tightly to his chest, his sleeves pushed up to reveal his beautiful, thick forearms. It's more clothes than he wore on the beach where he chose to go sans shirt, but even covered up, he's still delicious. Usually well put together, this morning his hair is mussed from sleep, and thick, black frames replace his normal contacts.

Daring to open my mouth, I speak when our eyes finally meet. "I...I'm sorry. I thought everyone had left for the day. I called out, but no one answered."

Colin's eyes reveal inner torment, like he is fighting some invisible battle, and I expect him to turn away, quickly retreat to his study, or even yell at me for my carelessness. Instead, with just a few large steps, he closes the distance between us, and with each rise of his chest, my arm, still tightly wrapped around my own body, brushes against the fabric of his shirt.

And then, one single finger reaches out, slowly tracing across my chest from shoulder to shoulder.

Holy. Fucking. Shit.

His large hand comes up to circle around my wrist before he gently pulls my arm away, baring my chest to his now hungry gaze. There is nothing tortured or tormented about him now. Instead, standing before me is a beast—a hungry wolf who has been hiding in sheep's clothing for entirely too long.

Still, his hand trembles when he brings it to my skin, lightly brushing the strands of my still-damp hair over my shoulder. I try to speak but am stunned into silence when ever-so-gently, Colin's lips dust over the thin skin that runs behind my ear.

He gingerly kisses his way down my arm before repeating the process on my other side, and when I realize what he is doing, kissing each and every one of my tattoos, I gasp.

Just when I think he is finished, he sinks to his knees in

front of me on the cold, kitchen floor, his hands reaching out to hold me by my hips. It's the absolute hottest fucking thing I have ever experienced in my life, and when his soft lips make contact with the sensitive skin of my hip, I grow infinitely wetter than I already was from the erotic ballet we seem to be performing with one another.

Studying Colin, I watch as he runs his nose across my body, inhaling deeply as he does. I watch as he takes in my favorite tattoo, as realization of what it says crosses his face, and relish in the small laugh he emits when he reads the candy hearts.

Making a motion for me to turn around, I obey, immediately missing the heat of his gaze. That heat is replaced by chills as one finger trails down the length of my spine before he's kissing the moons that line the center of my back.

He stands behind me for several long moments, and I begin to panic. When he finally returns to stand in front of me, I look away out of self-preservation, afraid of what I'll see reflected in his eyes. A finger creeps up the underside of my chin again, lifting my head up until I am able to meet his green eyes with mine. Dropping his hand from under my chin, the same hand reaches out to wrap around my arm, and before I can blink, I am pressed against his body.

This is it—the moment heroines in romance novels wait for their entire lives. And right now, in the kitchen of Colin's house, I'm living that moment.

He grinds against my naked body, the full-length of his erection pressing against me. With each roll of his hips, I can tell how hard he is and just how big he is. My hips meet his with each movement, and I can't help the needy sound that falls from my lips as one thrust skates right across the sensitive flesh between my legs.

His hands on my body, one weaves its way through my hair until he tugs on the strands tilting my head up...up...up until my eyes can meet his. As he holds my gaze, my pussy throbs despite the fact that both our hips are now still.

Over the last few months, I've talked to Colin more hours than I can count. I've talked to him first thing in the morning, last thing late at night, and every hour in-between. Yet, when he speaks now, his voice is unlike any I've ever heard from him. He's deep and raspy, all sorts of growly and sharp.

"You're fucking beautiful."

The words hit me between the thighs, now more than slick with my own arousal. I want to push him, just like I always do. I want to tease him with my body but also with my words.

As my lips quirk up into a smile, I turn on the heat with my eyes, making my words practically drip with sensuality as I tease the straitlaced single dad in front of me. "Colin Pappas! Did you just curse?"

Fingers still wrapped in my tangled hair, he tightens his grip to just the very edge of the pain-pleasure threshold I love, causing me to whimper into the quiet air between us. His voice is still gritty when he growls out in response, "Shut up, Little Girl."

Before I can retaliate, his lips are against mine with near bruising force. My hands ball up in the fabric of his shirt, bringing him even closer to me, and when he trails his tongue across my lips, I open up for him without hesitation. He leads our kiss with his hand still wrapped in my hair, the other sliding up and down my body. The tips of his fingers trail over the peaks of my breasts, his knuckles gently brushing over my sex, and he then wraps his arm around my body, roughly squeezing my ass cheek in his large palm, the tips of his fingers digging into my tender flesh.

Dizzy from the combination of his kisses and lack of oxygen, I pull away to stare at his chiseled face before I swipe my thumb across his bottom lip. I pull my own lip between my teeth, warring with how far I can push him before he scares.

It's stupid—so stupid—and I know he could shut this down at any second, that he could send me away or retreat on his own, but I can't help but ask, my breath coming out all soft when I say, "Take me to bed, Colin."

I'm afraid to look into his eyes, to see which version of the man I'm going to see when I peer into those emerald irises, but before I can look, he lifts me into his arms. My legs wrap around his torso, my arms around his neck, and as he carries me across the house, I can't help but nuzzle into his neck, rewarding him with tiny licks and bites along the way.

Wrapped around Colin's body as he carries me to my bedroom, I can't help but send up a silent prayer that this is actually happening, that it isn't all some silly sex dream I'm going to wake up from at any minute. I mean, I've dreamt about this day since the first time I laid eyes on Colin Pappas, but never in my wildest dreams did I ever expect them to come to fruition.

He kicks open the door, eyes briefly scanning the room as if checking for hidden monsters before he deftly walks us to the bed. Placing me in the middle of the plush mattress with my legs hanging over the side, I watch with rapt attention as he pushes my thighs apart before he lowers himself to his knees.

The heat radiating off my body is enough to melt the polar ice caps faster than global warming ever could. I need to feel his touch—either his hands or his mouth—but he doesn't touch me with either.

He simply stares at my center as if he's studying for an exam, memorizing every curve and each color and fold of my most sacred places.

"Colin..." I whimper his name, the desire burning in my very core most certainly coating my lips and slicking my thighs.

His eyes blaze dark as he breaks the spell and looks up the length of my body to meet my own. "You have no idea how long it's been since I've looked at a perfect, pink pussy. Do *not* rush me, Daphne."

Well, shit on a stick. Colin has a dirty mouth!

Colin's eyes roam south over my body again, his hands skating up my thighs with a quiet determination, and in this moment, he's all dark and demanding, giving more Daddy energy than I ever thought he would be capable of.

The pad of his thumb swipes through my center, the digit sliding easily through my wetness. He stops less than a centimeter away from my clit, and I momentarily want to scream into the silent room before he beings moving again, tracing my lips with the same wet digit, teasing me with tantalizing strokes along my folds but never touching the aching bundle of nerves between my legs.

"I've been dying to taste you for weeks, dying to touch your tight, little body, dying to feel your skin ignite under mine. I've thought about your mouth wrapped around my dick for months, thought about getting myself off with my cock wrapped around those little frilly panties of yours."

Where the hell has this man been hiding?

Lowering his head between my legs, his flat tongue takes one long, languid stroke up the length of my pussy. Starting at my entrance, he doesn't stop before he reaches my clit this time, and I moan at the contact. He pulls away just enough to speak. "Sweeter than the best whiskey I've ever tasted."

I can't stop my head from thrashing against the mattress when he returns to worshiping my pussy, alternating between long, full strokes, little bites and nibbles, and the perfect amount of suction. Colin flicks his tongue over my clit, and my eyes close, my lips parting.

"Christ, Colin! Please, don't stop!"

Two fingers easily slide inside me, and it's the best fucking sensation in the world as he works himself in and out while his tongue continues to swirl around my clit.

He slides out before returning on a groan, this time with three long, skilled fingers, and when he does, I correct my earlier thoughts because I know now that *this* is the best fucking thing in the world.

I miss the warmth of his tongue when he removes his mouth, though his fingers continue working me from the inside, even as he pushes himself up my body.

Pressing his mouth to mine, I taste myself on his lips, and I find myself licking at them, wanting to taste even more. Colin pulls away almost as swiftly as the kiss started, inching his way back down my body, stopping to kiss, lick, and nip along the way.

My body is on the precipice, a razor's edge away from tumbling into oblivion. I just need a little more. I thrust my hips along with the pace of his fingers, trying my hardest to get the slightest bit of pressure on my clit.

"Please," I beg him.

His teeth unclench from where they were sealed around my nipple. Slowly, he continues back down my body. "Are you going to be a good girl for me and wait to cum until my mouth is back on your pretty, little cunt?"

I admonish myself again because, fuck me, *this* is the best fucking sensation in the world—his lips on my body, his fingers inside of me, and his delightfully surprising naughty mouth asking me to be a good girl.

"Yes," I gasp. His mouth hovers above my pussy, the warm air of his breath whispering across my sensitive flesh. I want to thrust into him, to force his tongue back against my clit and to roll my pussy over his face again and again and again. "I'll be your good girl, Colin. I'll be whatever you want me to be as long as you let me cum."

Bracing myself for his mouth, I'm disappointed when it doesn't connect with my skin. Opening my eyes and peering down at him when he says my name, I find him in the same position—on his knees, still paused above me, but with his eyes trained on my face.

He pulls his fingers from me, and for a split second, I think I've lost him, that he's going to walk out of this room right now and never come back. That I'll be both alone *and* lonely.

Instead, he keeps his eyes on mine while he says with a voice full of desire, "Oh, Little Star. In here, you can call me *Daddy*."

Before I can respond, his fingers loudly sink back inside my cunt as his mouth connects with my clit, and with a few hurried strokes, I'm coming undone.

My vision oscillates between light and dark, my body trembling as wave after wave of my orgasm crashes through my soul. He continues to lick and suck, dragging out the pleasure I'm succumbing to. Sweat breaks out over my skin, and I'm panting as he continues to work me.

And though he gave me permission, I hesitate for a second before giving into the desire that has been forefront in my mind for months, yelling into the room, "Daddy, yes!"

Fourteen

COLIN

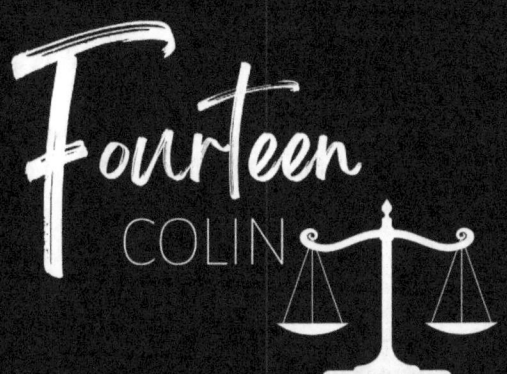

Damn, this woman is beautiful.

The little sprite arches off the mattress, her dark, raven hair splayed against the colorful quilt beneath her naked body as my fingers continue to slide in and out of her wet pussy.

I told her to call me Daddy, and she did. Hell, she didn't just call me Daddy, she yelled it into the room, her voice echoing off the four basic white walls surrounding us.

What I hadn't told Daphne was that I've been down the deepest of Google rabbit holes lately, devouring everything I could find about the lifestyle she lives. I learned terms like ageplay, caregiver, and brat. I found that many factors play into these relationships with everything from setting rules for her to follow, to punishing her when she disobeys them.

The more I found myself reading—pouring—over articles about common misconceptions of why people join the lifestyle, the more I wanted to learn.

And what was even more unexpected, when her voice rang out with what I once thought was a taboo term, I *liked* it.

I liked it so much that I almost came in my pants right there on my knees between her thighs as she coated my tongue with her sweet yet tangy taste.

Yeah, in less than twenty-four hours, this woman has almost made me cum...twice—without even touching me.

Now, as she catches her breath, legs still dangling off the edge of the mattress, I take a moment to scan her room, really taking in the eclectic collection of colorful tchotchkes and books that line the shelves. We were so hurried to get to the bed that I hadn't stopped to think of what being in here with her, like this, would feel like.

In the room that used to be mine. The room that I shared with Tabitha for years as we watched our perfect family blossom and grow around us. The room where we made love on the floor the first night we moved in, before any furniture had been delivered. The room where we fought about having more kids—her wanting to try again, me content with our two perfect daughters. The room we cried in together after her diagnosis, and the room I sobbed until I vomited in after she was gone.

The memories assault my senses, and I wait for the all-encompassing guilt to fill my chest, to stop my heart from beating, and make me flee back to the safety of my lonely, solitary life.

But it doesn't come.

"Colin?" Her voice is tentative and soft as it comes from where she is still laying.

Pushing up from my knees, I crawl onto the bed and settle down next to her slender frame. Pulling a blanket from the bed over her body, she turns to look at me, her beautiful, bright blue eyes darting back and forth between my own. I'm not sure what she sees or what she is expecting to find in my eyes, but whatever is there prompts her to ask. "Are...are you okay?"

A few strands of her hair have fallen over her round face,

and I gently swipe them behind her ear, running my knuckles over her cheek before bringing my hand back to myself. "Surprisingly, yeah."

Daphne smiles wide before carefully schooling her features. "Surprising because it was with me, or because of the whole Daddy thing, or..." She trails off on the last word, waiting for me to elaborate.

I just shake my head, not wanting to ruin what is happening between us with memories of the past, but Daphne pushes on. "Colin, I want to fuck you, like *really* want to fuck you—have for a long time. But I can't do that until I know that you'll enjoy it as much as I do. So, tell me what's going on in that big, beautiful brain of yours. Please."

Situating myself on my back, I stare at the ceiling, letting out a long sigh.

"This was my room with Tabitha for years. It wasn't until after she died that I moved upstairs, and when my mom moved out, I just stayed up there to be closer to the girls. I kept telling myself that it was so I could be there quickly after nightmares, that I could keep a closer eye on them as they grieved and healed, but I think I actually stayed there this entire time because it made me feel less alone to be closer to them. Hell, neither of them have even had a nightmare that ended in tears in over a year."

Daphne places a small palm against my chest, showing me compassion with her actions as well as her words. "I can't begin to imagine how hard it's been for you."

Placing my hand over hers, I trace small circles on the soft skin between her thumb and pointer finger. "I expected to feel disgusted after this."

Instantly, I backtrack, thinking about how bad that must have sounded to Daphne. "That didn't come out right. What I meant to say was that I expected to feel like I was cheating on

Tabitha, that I would be disgusted with myself for letting desire get the best of me."

"And...how do you feel?

"Honestly, last night I was angry with myself after how I acted. Hearing you call me Daddy and having you up against the wall—it was such a turn on that it freaked me out. Trust me when I say we'll be skipping pasta with red sauce for a few months in this house."

"Ewwww, Colin!" Daphne squeals, feigning shock. I retaliate by reaching over to grab her side, causing her to giggle and squeal even louder. When she finally calms back down, wiping a few stray tears that fell as she laughed, she turns her attention back to me. "So, what changed between last night and this morning?"

I pull her into my chest, inhaling her sweet, floral scent as it wafts from her now fully dry hair and into the space around us. "You're going to think I am ridiculous if I tell you."

Her small body pushes me flat on my back, surprising me with her strength, before she crawls on top of me, throwing a hip over each side of my pelvis. Daphne is still loosely wrapped in a blanket, but it doesn't block the heat radiating off her body as she straddles me.

"Have you even met me, Colin? I'm a grown-ass woman who likes to call men Daddy, has more stuffies than a six-year-old having a birthday party at fucking Build-A-Bear, and craves someone to make my decisions for me so I don't shut down and tailspin into an anxiety-induced tunnel. If I think anything you say is ridiculous, then you can call me a hypocrite and spank me until my ass turns nice and red."

Tugging the fabric wrapped around her body, I pull it away from her until she is bare to me. Running a hand up her smooth stomach, I stop to pinch both her nipples before continuing to skate up her neck, dipping my thumb into her mouth and dragging my damp finger across her bottom lip as I try to form words. "When I walked into the kitchen this morning and saw the way the light was hitting your body, through a window I hated for so long, a window my wife loved and begged me to keep—I...I felt like it was her way of giving me permission. That she was silently casting her approval on you and telling me it's time to move on with literal rays from the heavens. I've lived in this house for years. I've stood in that kitchen at almost every time of day, in every type of weather, and *never* has the sun created such a perfect beam of light."

Tears spring to her eyes and suddenly, I'm afraid that I said something wrong. Bringing my hands to her hips, hoping to keep her from moving away, I keep talking, in desperate need to tell someone else about the moment where I certainly—*finally* —got my life back.

"I could see flecks of dust dancing in the air as the sun hit them, but everything else in the room stood still around us as that light shone down onto your bare body. It was me and you, and in some way, it was Tabitha, too. I know that sounds so fucking deranged, Daphne, thinking my dead wife was in the room with us..." I trail off, huffing a self-deprecating laugh.

Tears fall fully now, sliding down her cheeks to spill onto my shirt below. "It's not deranged, Colin. It's not ridiculous or silly. It's more beautiful than you'll ever truly know."

Daphne leans over me, taking my lips with hers in a gentle, tentative kiss. "Thank you for letting me be part of this. For trusting me with your beautiful family and your even more beautiful heart. I know this is new for both of us, hell—I don't even know what *this* is. But no matter what this is, I never want to take her place. That's not me, Colin. I want you to talk about Tabitha, to tell me stories of your life together, to keep her memory alive and share those memories with me and the girls. I know you loved...*love* her deeply, and that doesn't have to stop just because you're now discovering that it is okay to be happy and fulfilled."

Tugging her to my chest, I wrap my arms tightly around her back, pressing a kiss to the top of her head as I ask, "How did you get to be so perfect, Little Star?"

Her lips stretch into a grin against my chest. "I don't know about perfect. I mean, from what I've been told, I have a *horrible* habit of leaving little panties in the most inconvenient places."

"Tell me the truth. Were you doing that on purpose the entire time?"

"The first time was an accident, I swear. But after that..." She trails off before breaking into a fit of giggles as I tickle her sides.

"I knew it, you little tease. There is no way in hell that one person can be so forgetful after so many not-so-gentle reminders."

Her hips squirm, and I realize that despite our initial deep topic of conversation, I am still primed and ready to go with an extremely sexy, naked woman on top of me. She cocks a perfectly arched eyebrow in my direction, and I roll my hips into her, groaning into the air at the same time she gasps.

Hands on my chest, Daphne lowers herself to my mouth, capturing my lips in a soft kiss before righting herself. "I think you secretly *like* when I tease you."

"Little Girl," I growl, "tease me or torment me; either way, you tempt me." Pulling her body back to my chest, I roll over, pinning Daphne below me. Reaching behind my back, I yank my shirt over my head, discarding it on the floor. It's not the first time she's seen me without my shirt on, but I can't help the ego boost I get whenever her eyes roam over my body. I might not have those coveted cuts that lead the way to the jackpot like my best friend does, and I've been rocking more of a four-and-a-half-pack for the last ten years, but the way her blue eyes study my chest make me feel like I'm in college all over again.

Sliding my pants over my hips, I push them down before shimmying them over my legs, adding them to the pile of clothes on the floor. Fisting my cock, I give it several slow strokes before urging Daphne to part her legs.

Settling between her thighs, I tease her pussy with the head of my dick, slowly dragging it through her wet folds and over her sensitive clit. Again and again, I run myself through her lips, coating myself in her wetness with each swipe of my cock. Every time, inching closer to her entrance and every time evading the place she most wants me to be.

I want to tease her as badly as she has been teasing me.

Torment her as badly as she has been tormenting me.

"Colin, please!"

Instead of stopping, I place myself at her entrance and push just the head of my cock inside. I glance down at the erotic sight, twitching against the heat of even the slightest contact with her center. "I don't know, Little Star. You sound so pretty begging for it that I almost want to keep this up."

Daphne tries to move her hips, to bring me further inside her cunt, but I keep my hands firmly wrapped around her hips, preventing her from finding the relief she seeks.

A pathetic, needy mewl rumbles from somewhere within her body as I feed her the next inch of my cock. "Barely inside of you, and I can already tell how tight your little pussy is going to be for me."

One more inch slides inside her body, and I watch as Daphne's eyes flutter shut with the movement. Finally removing one hand from her hip, I run it up her stomach before spreading it out over her breast. I've never had a preference when it comes to a woman's chest, but this woman has proven the adage that good things—great things, actually—really do come in extremely small packages.

"Open your eyes, baby." I reward her with another inch of my dick when she complies. My eyes bounce between her face and the place where we are joined, not sure which I am more fascinated with.

"You said before that you like to call men Daddy."

Another inch sinks inside.

"But if we're doing this, if we're going to be together and we're really going to try for something real..."

I pull all the way out, lock eyes with Daphne, and hold her still with only my gaze. "Then I'm the only fucking man you'll be calling Daddy from now on."

This time, I don't tease. I don't torment or even tempt.

No, this time, I slide all the way home.

My hands are on her body, and she moves under me, yet I still take a minute to memorize every single aspect of this moment, afraid I'll wake up at any minute and be left alone again. I bask in the way her breath hitches when I angle my hips and slide deeper into her cunt. I study the way her perfect breasts bounce with each thrust. I commit every gasp and moan to memory, filing them away to access while I'm on my deathbed, as the best moments of my life flash before my eyes.

Because Daphne—she's *that* fucking good.

She's good and pure, like a light summer breeze against your skin.

"I want you on top of me."

Lazily, she smiles at me, still gyrating her hips to meet mine. "Then you better put me on top of you, Colin."

Good and pure, yes—but still as defiant as ever.

The perfect mixture of sugar and spice.

"Keep sassing me, baby. That bratty mouth of yours is going to get you in trouble." Leaning over her body, I crush my lips to hers. We lick into each other's mouths, and with one hand under her head, the other under her back, I roll, keeping our lips locked together as the scent of our mingling pleasure fills the air around us.

Wasting no time, Daphne pushes away from my chest and moves her hips. She runs her hands up the sides of her own body before running her fingers through her hair. Piling the tresses on the top of her head and holding them away from her body, she continues to rock back and forth. "I'm on top of you, *baby*," she imitates me when she says the word. "Now what?"

My hands find her hips, already knowing it's one of their new favorite places. "Now I'm going to fuck you until you soak my cock, and then I'm going to explode in that tight, little cunt of yours."

"Never in my wildest dreams did I think you'd have such a filthy mouth," she retorts.

"Want to keep talking about my mouth, or do you want me to actually fuck you now?" I thrust my hips between her thighs, just once, and she groans in response.

"Fuck me, please."

I give her a smile, a small sign of praise. "Good girl, using your manners. Now hold on, Little Star. We're about to come undone together."

She drops her hands to my chest, balancing herself with my body as I begin to pump into her. With every thrust of my hips from beneath her, she comes down on me from the top. Over and over and over again, we meet in the middle, the only sounds in the room coming from our skin and the sounds of our combined, building pleasure.

Finding my way between us with one hand, I press my thumb to her clit, applying enough pressure to have Daphne dropping her head to the space between my shoulder and neck. She's wet, absolutely soaked, and I easily slide back and forth along the sensitive flesh. Panting into my skin, she moans—a guttural and throaty sound that comes from deep within.

"That's it, baby. Let me hear you come undone. Let me feel you."

I thrust harder—faster—while continuing to rub her clit.

"You feel *so* good." She croons the words on a breathy exhale. "I'm...I'm *so* close."

"Let go, baby. I'll be right there with you."

Less than a minute later, she's coming undone—squeezing my cock and milking me with her pussy as she yells my name.

And just like I promised her, I'm right there with her.

It starts at the base of my spine, the electricity rapidly moving throughout my entire body. I keep thrusting, even with Daphne's now limp body on top of mine. Using what muscle I have, I sit up and hold her to my chest as I pump, and pump, and pump before I spill into her, a roar leaving my mouth.

We stay wrapped in one another's arms for several quiet moments. Daphne's body trembles against mine, and I reach for the earlier discarded blanket wrapping it around her before carefully sliding out of her body. It's only in this minute that I notice exactly how much I feel like her protector right now, and just how much that role appeals to my soul.

Fifteen

DAPHNE

Ignoring the alarm blaring from the other side of my room, I take a moment to stretch in bed, reveling in the delicious soreness radiating from between my thighs. The funky pink and orange patterned sheets are cool against my skin, while a sun catcher casts a rainbow of colors onto the floor around me.

I had sex with Colin yesterday.

Actually, I had a lot of sex with Colin yesterday.

We had sex on my bed, on the floor of my room, against the refrigerator when we went to heat up leftovers for lunch, in the shower, and then in my bed again—all before Emily made it home from school.

All day, I kept waiting for him to run away, to flee to the safety of the gym in the garage or to his office where he would bury his face in legal briefs and emails, but that moment never happened. In fact, it's like he was suddenly insatiable, unable to keep his hands off me much in the way I couldn't take mine off his gorgeous body.

He surprised me in all the very best ways.

Colin surprised me after I had a post-round-one-freak-out because we didn't use protection—when he told me we were okay, that he had a vasectomy close to ten years ago after he and Tabitha decided not to try for another child. From what he told me, it was a rare point of contention in their marriage for several years after the fact, one of the few times they didn't fully see eye-to-eye.

Then he surprised me again after round three—after he had me pinned to the refrigerator, coaxing multiple orgasms out of me as he told me I was his precious, good girl. He confessed while we ate sandwiches, naked on the kitchen floor, that he had been educating himself on the Daddy and little girl dynamic and confided in me that the idea turned him on. What started as a tentative confession turned into a full-on conversation, where we talked about what appeals to each of us about the lifestyle. Colin told me the idea of protecting me and helping me make decisions spoke to his nurturing side but that navigating this new potential identity is something he wants to do *correctly*. When I asked him what he meant by correctly, he simply asked that I give him seventy-two hours and that I'd know. Of course, intrigued in the very best way possible, I agreed without hesitation.

But of all the surprises, the biggest came when Colin shook me to my core—quietly knocking on my door after Emily had gone to sleep for the night. Taking my lips with his, I welcomed his gentle kiss, reveling in the way his hands slowly roamed my body before he tiptoed back upstairs to his own suite only after whispering, "Goodnight, Little Star," into my ear.

It was intimate and loving, a silent vow promised with his lips—the vow to cherish me and care for me, to adore me and hopefully to one day *love* me.

Finally pulling myself out of my plush bed and the

daydream of memories of the two of us together, I cross the room to turn off the alarm. I catch a glimpse of myself in the mirror that hangs over the large, white dresser. The giant, silly grin that I fell asleep with on my face last night is still plastered there this morning. For once, after seeing the pure happiness on my face, it doesn't even bother me that unlike most people, I have to go to extremes to get myself out of bed in the morning.

Of course, I couldn't be the type of girl who can just reach over to her nightstand and turn off her morning alarm. Nope. Not me. I'd slap that sucker to turn on the snooze feature and wake up three hours later with drool stuck to my face while wondering what day of the week it was.

I all but bounce through my late-morning routine, a lightness in my step as I shower, pull on a Broken Sparrow tee, and pack a light lunch for myself. In my car, I make a quick detour to Dina's Diner before pulling into my usual parking spot at the studio.

The small bell above the door chimes, signaling my entrance, while Raven greets me with a smile full of perfectly straight, white teeth from behind the front desk. She looks back and forth between the paper bag in my hands and my face a few times, seeming to study me with suspicious eyes before squealing into the quiet, vacant shop, "You had sex last night!"

Thankful that our first customers of the day haven't arrived yet, I still can't help but chastise her as my eyes dart around for my best friend. "Shhhh, it's a sensitive subject."

Just as I finish my sentence, I hear my aforementioned best friend as she appears from the office, an ever-present large coffee in hand. "Who had sex? It sure as hell isn't me this week, my period has turned me into a..." She trails off as she gives me a once over.

Raven's head volleys between the two of us as if she is watching a tennis match, waiting for one of us to make a move.

Shoving the bag into Mina's hands, I take a step back. "I brought you peanut butter pie," I say in a singsong voice.

She eyes me suspiciously.

"Did I mention how beautiful you look today? How lucky I am to have you in my life? How much I appreciate you and love you?" Backing up further, I put a rack of merchandise between us.

Mina laughs, her lips tipping up into a smile. "I've been wondering when you two would crack. But trying to butter me up with pie and compliments? That's just low, Daph." Turning to look at Raven, she points a plum-painted nail in her direction. "This one is all you, girl. I have no desire to talk to my best friend about her sleeping with my brother."

Raven screams with laughter as Mina tucks into the bag, pulling out a large slice of pie and a plastic fork.

"Noooooo," I whine. "I need my girl!"

Pointing to Raven with her fork as she juggles the thick slice of pie and her coffee mug, Mina retorts, "You've got her right there. If there is one thing in this life I don't ever want to think about, it's Colin having sex."

I let out a contented sigh, the memories of his very naked body flashing through my mind before I turn my attention back to Mina, who is walking toward the office. "Just promise me you're not mad at me?"

She turns and gives me a genuine smile that reaches her kind, green eyes. Mina and Colin share the same color—that deep bottle green. But while Colin's eyes hold reverence and respect for those around him, Mina's hold mischief and a dash of sass.

"Nah, girl. I'm not mad at all. Actually, I'm excited for the both of you. I just absolutely do *not* want to know if or how you got my brother to agree to let you call him *Daddy*."

Gasping, I turn to face Raven, my face heating as my best

friend unintentionally spills some of my secrets. "Don't listen to anything she says. She doesn't know what she's talking about!"

Raven simply shrugs, not missing a beat. "I'm a polyamorous pansexual who enjoys group play and pegging men. Who the hell am I to judge what anyone does in their bedroom? Now get over here and give me all the delicious details."

Twenty minutes later, my new confidant has been filled in on my growing feelings for my best friend's brother—and none of the sexiest details are left out of the story. I tell Raven about the panties, the day at the beach where things shifted between us, the light flirting, and finally, I tell her *all* about yesterday.

Jumping down from where I have been perched on the black reception desk, I turn toward the sound of the tinkle from the shop's bell, expecting to be met by my first appointment of the day. Instead, familiar green eyes stare back at me, a shy smile playing across his lips.

Raven glances between us with a huge grin that can only be described as shit-eating. Then, she quietly makes herself scarce before Colin advances further into the shop. All business today, he's dressed in a pair of slim-cut dress pants that hug his lower half and a crisp, white button-up shirt. A deep purple tie—so dark it is almost black—hangs loosely around his neck and I'm not ashamed to admit I think of him using that tie to bind my wrists behind my back while he has his way with my body.

I meet him halfway, a giddy feeling coursing through my body. Like when you're in high school and your crush catches your eye from across a crowded cafeteria, my belly flutters and my heart picks up speed.

"Hey, you," I breathe out.

Colin reaches out, tucking a stray strand of hair behind my ear. "Is it okay? That I came to see you?"

"Yeah, I...um...told your sister. Or, well, she kind of guessed." I bite my lower lip, sounding nervous when I speak.

He tugs on my lower lip, releasing it from where I had it between my teeth before glancing around the room to make sure we're alone. Leaning into me, his hot breath tickles the shell of my ear. "Told her that I fucked you like the dirty, little girl you are, or told her that we're going to try for something real?"

Colin's words send small bolts of electricity straight to my core, the tingles radiating out from that central place within me. "That dirty mouth of yours is going to get you in trouble talking to me like that in the middle of the day. Speaking of which, to what do I owe the pleasure of this midday visit?"

Pressing his lips to mine, he grins into the quick, chaste kiss. "I'm on my way back to my office, but I wanted to ask if I could take you out for dinner tonight?"

"What about Emily?" I ask, wrapping my arms around his waist, loving the way he fits against me, loving that I get to have my hands on his body, that I get to have *him*. His body is all hard planes and muscle. It's not lost on me that not only is Colin a total Daddy, but he's actually one hell of a *Zaddy*.

I'm a very lucky girl.

Colin tilts my chin up...up...up until I'm finally able to look into his eyes. "Here I am asking you on a proper date, and your first thought is about my kid. You're one hell of a woman, Daphne."

This time, his kiss is anything but quick. It's not sloppy, but it's not pretty as we lick and nip at each other's lips like two hungry animals feasting after a long hibernation. One of his hands fists in my hair as the other lands on my hip. Outside the floor to ceiling windows that make up the front of the shop, people walk by, unaware of the flames burning us alive within.

From behind us, a voice rings out, "Damnit, guys! Just

because I'm comfortable with the two of you doing whatever it is you're doing doesn't mean that I want to see it in Technicolor!"

We break apart like two teenagers caught by their parents, but Colin quickly pulls me back into the warmth of his arms, my back to his chest. "Like I haven't had to deal with you and my best friend for the last few years. Consider it payback, dear sister." His tone is light—dare I say *playful*—and it fills me with so much joy to see him slowly emerging from his grief-stricken shell. "And if you *must* know, dear sister—what we're doing is dating. Exclusively."

Although we had talked in the heat of the moment about being exclusive, hearing him say it now sends little tingles down my spine. My cheeks hurt from smiling at his words, and when I look at my best friend, I almost cry when I see that she is smiling too.

"Honestly, you guys look cute together. It's disgusting." Mina rolls her eyes at us in a playful way, and I giggle in response. "Guess your plan to keep her in your house worked out for the best, Colin."

He stiffens behind me, his hands dropping away from my body. Turning to look at his face, I notice he's gone pale, looking as if he has seen a ghost.

"Oh, fuck," my best friend groans out, her hands coming up to rub at her temples. "You never told her?"

"Told me what?" I ask.

Colin speaks next, his voice heavy. "I was waiting until the time was right."

"Colin! You can't keep something like that to yourself!" Mina exclaims.

"Told me what?" I repeat louder, hoping one of the two of them will tell me what the fuck is going on and what it has to do with me.

Finally, they stop playing the parts of bickering siblings and look at me. Colin breaks the silence, taking my hands in his as he does. "It was something I wanted to talk to you about tonight, and I would understand if it changes your feelings about me." He looks guarded, almost pained. "My sister and Nico's place has been ready for a while. I asked that they not share that information with you."

I'm not angry, but I am confused as I ask softly, "Why would you do that?"

Mina slowly backs out of the room, leaving us alone at the front of the shop. "I wasn't ready to let go of you. Having you in the house with me, with the girls and the dog and everything else that comes with it—it made me feel like I was part of a team again.

"And then, every day, we got closer, and suddenly, it was like I was becoming *me* again. The me who could feel things, the me who *wanted* to feel things. If you left, if you moved out —hell, I was terrified that I would lose that. I'm *still* terrified of that. Tell me this doesn't change anything between us, Little Star. Please tell me this doesn't change us?"

I shake my head, reaching up to cup his cheek in my palm while hating the pained look on his face. "I feel like I should be angry. That I should feel like you went behind my back and withheld information from me, but in all honesty, I don't feel that way at all. I kinda feel honored that you didn't kick me out after the first week."

He reaches down and tickles my sides. I squeal, trying to break free. "Don't think I didn't think about it in those first few weeks."

I feign a bullet to the chest, dramatically gasping. "How dare you ever had such horrendous thoughts!"

I'm in his arms again, one hand cupping the back of my head as he breathes in my scent. "Thank you for not being mad at me. I know I'm going to mess this up at least another hundred times, but know I'll always be trying my damnest to do right by you."

"You had the best of intentions, however flawed they may have been. Just promise me that going forward, you let me be part of the conversation. I know I've asked you to make decisions for me in the past and that I'm comfortable with giving up a lot of control, but I still want to be part of the narrative of those decisions. Especially when they impact my life. But don't worry, you can make up for it with that dinner you came in to ask about."

We part ways after making plans when my first client comes in and I find myself counting down the hours until I get to see him again.

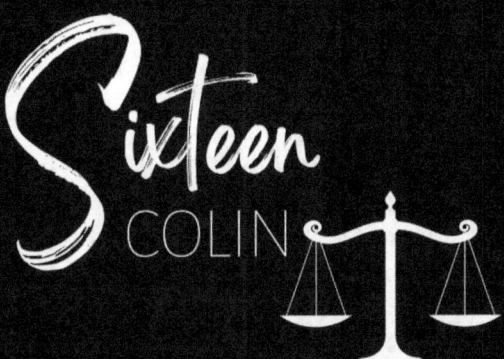

Sixteen
COLIN

Ringing your own doorbell has to be one of the strangest feelings in the world, but when you live with the woman you want to impress, it's necessary to get a little creative.

I hear her movements as she grows closer before the large, wooden door opens. In an instant, I forget how to speak. I forget that I have an oversized bouquet of flowers in my hands. I forget that I should pull her into a hug or press my lips to hers or tell her how beautiful she looks.

Daphne wears a strapless cocktail dress that hits just above her knees. It's as black as her raven hair that now cascades around her shoulders in gentle curls, and it's almost as luminous as those soft strands. A bubblegum pink pair of heels adorn her feet, giant bows tied on each ankle dwarfing her already small stature. Her eyelids are swept with a smoky shadow, lips glossy and pink and perfectly kissable.

"Colin?" she asks, dragging my name out into several long syllables. "What are you doing out here?" Daphne looks around as if expecting someone else to be outside the front door.

Finally gaining some composure, I clear my throat before speaking. "I'm here to pick you up for our date. These are for you."

Reaching out to take the bouquet from my hands, Daphne beams at me. "Why don't you come in for a minute so I can put these in some water, then we can go."

I follow her into the kitchen, where she finds a vase under the sink that I never knew existed. Shaking the included plant food packet into the bottom, she fills it up with water before snipping the stems and adding them to the mixture. Setting them proudly in the center of the island, she turns to me, a distant emotion flitting across her gorgeous face. "No one has ever gotten me flowers before."

Not being able to help myself, I pull her into my arms and place a tender kiss on the top of her head, loving the way she smells like a summer rainstorm tonight—all fresh and warm despite the recently cooler fall temperatures. "That's because you've only dated boys before."

"You saying you're not one?" I can feel her grin against my chest.

"No, baby. I'm saying I'm a man." I lower my hands, grabbing a handful of her ass. "Now let's get going before I drag you to your bedroom and we miss our reservation. That dress looks stunning on you, and it's going to take some serious self-restraint to behave with you looking deliciously sinful."

She doesn't protest, instead grabbing her small clutch purse from atop the counter. "As much as I'd love to stay in bed with you all night, I'm really enjoying the way you fill out that gorgeous shirt and wouldn't mind that view for a few more hours first. Your initials embroidered on the cuffs somewhere?"

I bark out a sharp laugh, loving her teasing and feeling

thankful that she has chosen me out of all the men in the world. "You're a crazy woman," I holler after her retreating form.

She turns back around, tossing a wink in my direction. "Only crazy for you, Casanova."

We arrive at the restaurant about a half hour later, an upscale steakhouse the next town over. I've never been here before, but after a quick consult with both my sister and my best friend via the most awkward group text ever, I learned that not only is steak basically a food group to Daphne but that she had mentioned wanting to come here after Mina told her how delicious their menu was.

I open the car door for Daphne, extending my hand to help her out of the vehicle—another move I'm sure she has never had done for her in the past. Seriously, where has she been finding the boys she's been dating?

"I've been wanting to come here since I moved to town!"

"I know," I reply. "I may have had a little bit of help planning this on such short notice. I know I was initially apprehensive that you are my sister's best friend, but it's been nothing but beneficial thus far."

The blonde hostess ushers us through the main dining room to a second, smaller room that is flanked with rich, round, velvety red booths. All around us, dark wood tones cover the walls and flooring while crisp, white linens sit atop the tables.

Handing a menu first to Daphne and then to myself, the hostess excuses herself, leaving us in the quiet din of the diners around us. Reaching out, I pluck the menu from between Daphne's fingers where it has remained unopened. "Would you like me to order for you?"

"Yes, please." Two words spoken with such emotion behind them. She speaks them softly, but a current of gratitude still weaves around the consonants and vowels that make up those two simple words.

"How do you like your steak cooked?"

Daphne smiles, the small crow's feet around her eyes making her even more irresistible. "Knock off its horns and wipe its ass and I'm good to go."

I chuckle. "My kind of woman."

We both know I'm not only talking about how she likes her steak prepared.

When our server appears, I order for both of us before quickly turning back to Daphne. "I know I asked for seventy-two hours, but I'm ready to talk tonight. Talk about what it means to do this correctly. I have absolutely no clue how any of this is supposed to go." I give a small, self-deprecating laugh. "I mean, I'm not insecure in my masculinity. I can admit to watching that *Fifty Shades of Grey* movie, but that's not real life. I am a lawyer though, so if you do want a true contract, that can be arranged."

"A contract?" She drags the word out, like she isn't sure she heard me correctly.

"Yeah, you know," I take a quick look around, making sure our conversation will not be overheard, "defining your age play and my role as your Daddy. Our rules, rewards, and punishments. Talking about your limits and safe words..."

Daphne slides a little closer to me. "You really have been doing your research."

"I want to be the man you deserve."

We pause our conversation when our server returns with our beverages, Daphne only speaking when the young man again retreats. "Colin, you already are. But I need to ask you something, and I only want the truth."

I nod in her direction, urging her to continue with her question.

"Does this lifestyle actually turn you on, or are you doing

this strictly to please me? We don't have to do this for me to want you in my life."

"I never thought it would appeal to me," I answer honestly, taking the time to think about my words before I speak. "But it does. I don't know if it is something deep inside that I always would have come to enjoy because it was programmed into my DNA or if it is because it's an extension of who you are and I want nothing more than to make you happy. It's about bringing you happiness and making you feel safe, and damn if both of those things don't turn me on nearly as much as your body does."

She blushes, and she does it so rarely that it is even cuter than it should be.

"That means the world to me, Colin. Also, don't think that I missed your confession to watching *Fifty Shades of Grey*. Count on me holding onto that tidbit of information until just the right time."

She's sitting close to me in the round booth, and I playfully nudge her, loving that I get to have her this close to me after all the weeks of slow torture. "What? Going to tell me that the book was better?"

"Honestly, it wasn't," she confesses with a laugh. "You want something that depicts a true representation of the kink community, I can absolutely point you in the right direction, but that atrocity was not it."

Fresh bread is deposited on our table, and without thinking about it, I reach for a piece, smoothing cool butter over its warm surface, watching as it melts into the flaky dough. Placing the bread on Daphne's small plate, I then reach for another piece and repeat the process for myself.

"You're a natural caregiver," she says before tearing a piece of the bread and popping it into her mouth. "But, circling back to your question, no, we don't need a contract. Some people in alternative lifestyles do use one, but it's more for the people involved as opposed to something truly binding. Plus, I find that our roles can change so frequently, that the only true way to make sure we stay on the same page and remain confident in our relationship is to stay in constant, honest communication with one another."

We talk briefly about rules and rewards as we eat our salads, touching on topics like punishment, *funishment*, and the difference between the two. I never thought I would be having a serious discussion with a beautiful woman over dinner about the prospect of picking out her panties each day or spanking her when she disobeys me, but here we are.

And it's turning me on.

Over our next course, a braised beef and pesto flatbread which we share, we talk about limits and safe words. Daphne giggles at me when I tell her I don't think we'll ever need one, or rather, that I would be the one to need them more than she would.

"You'd be surprised," she says with a casual air of nonchalance.

"Have you had to use yours in the past?" I ask, truly curious of her answer.

"A few times. It was never for anything super bad or wrong. Once, I just got a really bad case of the giggles. They took me out of the scene so completely that I couldn't be present in a safe way, so I safe worded before we even started. Other than that, a few times early in my exploration when partners went a little too heavy during impact play, but I learned to be more discerning about my partners as I grew into the community."

"Can I ask you another question?"

She reaches out, lacing our fingers together on the tabletop. "You can ask me anything you want. This is that communication I was talking about. Also," she gives my hand a little squeeze, "it's a huge turn on to watch you as you learn and get to experience all of this."

I squeeze back, apprehensive about my next question but needing to know the answer. "How many other men have you been like this with?"

Daphne doesn't hesitate. "Two. I've had two partners that I've entered into long-term dynamics with. One is a wonderful man who I met—hell, probably close to fifteen years ago at this point. We're still friends, and I would catch up with him and his now-wife a few times each year while I was living in Portland. I was even in their wedding party. The other, well, let's just say it ended very badly for both parties involved."

I know what event she is referring to but decide not to push on what limited information she tells me about that second man. She'll tell me when she is ready, and when she does, I'll be there to support her in any way she needs from me.

Our entrees are delivered, and as Daphne reaches for her fork and knife, I steady her hand with mine. "Let me take care of that for my Little Girl."

Her body melts against the velvet material of the booth, and I catch a glimpse of her thighs as her dress inches up her legs. I take time to trail my gaze up her body to her stunning smile. "You're already the best Daddy I've ever had."

Once her steak is cut into bite-sized pieces, I stab one with her fork before dragging it through the thick, red wine demi-glaze lining the dinner plate. Bringing it to her lips, I watch with rapt attention as she parts her pink pout before closing her lips around the tines. Sliding the fork from her mouth, she moans as she bites into the meat, and my cock jerks in reply. A small dab of sauce sits just outside the corner of her lips, and I reach out to swipe it away, my dick growing even harder when she captures my thumb with her mouth and licks it clean.

"Keep that up, Little Star, and we won't make it through the rest of this meal."

Daphne bites her lower lip before picking up her fork and eating another piece of her meal. When she returns her gaze to me, her eyes are blazing. "Sex in public. Hard limit or soft limit?"

"It's not something I've ever done before, but not something that completely turns me off—so, I guess a soft limit. Then again, I'm also a lawyer, and that's something I sure as hell don't want to get caught doing."

We eat as we continue to talk, each question becoming more and more of a turn-on as we go. She finishes her meal, and I praise her for being a good girl before ordering her chocolate cake for dessert—which she devours while making delicious little noises.

Only when we're back in the car do we turn the conversation to my daughters. "What about the girls?" Daphne asks.

"What about them?" I respond, confused by the change in subject.

"Do you want to hide us from them? I mean, obviously they don't need to know that their dad is spanking me when I don't watch my mouth, but like...the fact that we're dating."

I pull her as close as I can get her in the car and kiss her long and deep. Pulling away is painful; all I want to do is keep my lips on hers. "No, Daphne. I don't want to hide us from anyone. Not the girls, not my mom. You're too precious to hide away behind closed doors."

She gasps, and I swear her eyes go misty as she cups my scruff-covered cheek with her hand. "You're such a remarkable man. I swear, I've never felt so close to someone and so cherished so damn fast. It's beautiful and scary all at the same time."

I smile at her, a soft smile that reaches my eyes. It's a smile

I've had on my face more since she came into my life. A smile that was missing for a long time, and a smile that feels so damn good to feel again. "Want to tell them together next weekend when Laurel is home on fall break?"

"Afraid you're going to need backup?" she chides.

"Hell yeah, I am. You might not terrify me, Little Girl, but two teenagers against their dad? I'm already shaking."

Daphne laughs in response, sliding our fingers together as I drive us back toward Johnson Creek and my home.

No, not my home.

Our home.

Because at this minute—at this absolute second—I know I'm never letting her go, no matter how long it takes to say the words she deserves to hear.

Seventeen
DAPHNE

Leaves float down from the trees in various shades of reds, oranges, and yellows, covering the usually pristine backyard. I gaze out of the kitchen windows, watching as Stella tromps around, chasing random leaves and crashing into neatly-raked piles. Colin, Laurel, and Emily laugh while working in tandem as I watch with rapt attention, loving how happy he looks to have both of his daughters back under the same roof—even if just for a few days.

Mama Pauli darts around the kitchen, chopping and mincing vegetables before heating an oversized wok that she brought from her condo. While she hasn't started the actual cooking yet, I can already imagine the smells that will soon be wafting through the space, all garlicky and gingery. There is no better feeling than walking into the house after work on a Friday to discover what she has already been cooking for hours, taking a few minutes to guess the spices and scents in the air before Pauli reveals what's on the weekly menu. It's a brief moment of my week, but one that makes me feel closer to my own mother, closer to the moments when it was just her and I alone in the kitchen where we would bake together, her always letting me sneak extra treats as often as she could.

Tonight, she's treating us to the newest recipes she has learned in her cooking class—homemade egg rolls along with lo mein, a vegetable stir fry, and orange chicken.

Mina and Nico arrive, letting themselves into the house. Nico gives welcoming hugs to me and Pauli before heading out back, picking up Emily to toss her into the leaves. We take a minute to stare out the window in unison, Pauli looking on in adoration at her son and granddaughters while Mina and I look longingly at the two beautiful men who have captured each of our hearts.

Because of the weather, we have moved our Friday tradition into the large dining room that lays to the left of the kitchen. An oversized, white, wooden table runs down the middle of the room. Flanked with chairs on three sides, the fourth side features a bench that runs the entire length of the table. It's large, yet cozy, not feeling pretentious or too large for the space. One wall features built-in cabinets and is filled with what I can only assume is the good China—the kind that only gets pulled out for holidays and special occasions. All I know is that we've never used it in my time here.

We're all seated, various bowls and serving platters being passed around, while Laurel regales us with stories of her life at college. I notice Colin flinching beside me as she mentions the same boy for the third time, and I reach out a hand to give his thigh a small, yet reassuring squeeze beneath the table—away from the eyes of everyone sitting around us.

Once everything is served and the conversation lowers to a more manageable level, Colin clears his throat, and I immediately know what is coming. Now, it's my time to flinch, nervously aware that he's not only about to tell his daughters that we're dating, but his mom and best friend, too. Although, if I'm being honest, I wouldn't be surprised if Mina already told Nico. My best friend is more than capable of many things, but secret keeping usually isn't one of them. She's the type of girl who would find her Christmas presents, unwrap them to see what's inside, and rewrap them with enough precision that no one would ever bat an eye.

Love the girl to death, but she's a sneaky little bitch.

With all eyes on Colin, he takes my hand under the table before speaking. "I'm glad you're all here tonight. I know Friday dinners are normal for us, but I've actually been wanting to talk to you all about something, and this seemed like the perfect opportunity." I give his hand a little squeeze, and with that movement, he pulls our linked hands from beneath the table, placing them where everyone can see them in the open. Eyes dart between our hands and our faces from all sides of the table, while Mina sits with a little smile as she watches her brother. "It's taken time, lots of time actually, but I've made the decision that I'm ready to open up again. Ready to start living my life as more than the shell I've been for the last few years."

His voice is shaky and laced with emotion as he continues. "You all know how much I loved...*love* Tabitha. Nothing will ever replace her in my heart. But then, something unexpected happened." He looks over at me with a wide smile that punches me in the gut while our fingers remain laced together on the tabletop. "Or rather, someone unexpected."

Colin doesn't get to continue, his girls bursting into hoots and hollers from the bench seat across the table. All around the table, we're met with a chorus of "finally" and "about times."

I beam up at him, so proud to see the happiness and support from his family, and he smiles back wider, leaning down to whisper in my ear while everyone else continues to chatter about our news. "I guess we were the last two to see it."

"Nah, just you," I tease. "I knew you'd come to your senses at some point."

Movement across the table catches my eye, and when I manage to tear my gaze away from Colin, I see various ones, fives, and even a ten-dollar bill piling up in the middle of the table. Confused, I ask, "What are you guys doing?"

No-one stops, instead passing bills back and forth.

"Who had today?" Nico hollers at Laurel, who pulls her phone out of her pocket.

The teen swipes on her screen a few times before her eyes scan whatever is now on the screen. "Um...looks like Nana is closest without going over."

Dissatisfied groans erupt around the dining room, while Pauli lets out a satisfied yelp, seemingly delighted with whatever game it is she just won.

Colin and I sit in stunned silence, eyes darting between our loved ones. Finally, he breaks the spell the rest are under. "You guys were betting on when I would start dating again?"

"Dad, no. We were betting on when you would start dating Daphne!" It's Emily who speaks up first, talking through a fit of giggles as Pauli reaches out to the pile of cash, grabbing it to count her winnings. "We all knew she was perfect for you."

Between the two of us, we must field a thousand questions through the rest of our meal, and when I excuse myself from the table to help Pauli carry in dishes, she pulls me into a hug, warmer and full of more love than she has ever shown me before. "He is a fantastic man, Daphne. Please take care of him, and I know he'll always do the same in return. You're showing him how to live again, that it's all worth it. I know because I was the same way after my husband died. I've watched my son walk around in a fog for years now, and while I can say without a doubt that I never expected him to end up with someone as colorful and carefree as you, I can say that I am thrilled that you are the woman he chose to start the next chapter of his life with."

I hold onto her tighter, grinning even as my throat tightens and my eyes mist. "I don't know if Colin or Mina have ever told you, but I lost my mom young—I was only seven. I still miss her every day. Miss what little bits and pieces I remember about growing up with her by my side."

Letting go of Pauli, I wipe the few stray tears that managed to fall. "Being here—and not just being here with my best friend or being here with the man I've fallen for—but being in this house with the girls and Stella, having you here every week, it feels like I belong for the first time in a very long time. It feels like I'm...*home*."

"Thank you for sharing that with me, dear. That must have been rough at such a young age."

"It was. It caused me to grow up fast and I missed out on a lot of what other kids my age were doing. But it also taught me to value family, those we have by birth *and* those we choose. Having you as part of my found family," my voice cracks when I try to continue, "it really means the world to me."

We hug again, not separating until Colin joins us in the kitchen. "Everything okay in here?"

"Yeah, we were taking bets on where you will take me for our first anniversary," I playfully tease.

I'm rewarded with a small laugh as Colin pulls me into his arms, while looking pointedly at his mom. "Speaking of bets, how much did you make off of my years of pain and suffering?"

She shrugs nonchalantly. "I managed to come out with thirty-seven bucks. It's going right into my Bingo fund."

"You play Bingo?"

"Almost every week at the Elk's Lodge. I've been trying to get Philly to come with since she moved home."

"Oh we're totally going! With her or without her!"

"You've got yourself a date. I'll send you a text with the upcoming dates, and you let me know whenever you're free."

Carrying dessert and mugs filled with freshly-brewed coffee, the three of us return to the dining room, where we finish out our weekly family meal with loud conversation, embarrassing stories, and promises to do it all again next week.

And while this isn't the first time I've had Friday night dinner with them, far from it actually, it is the first time I *truly* feel like part of their family.

Eighteen
COLIN

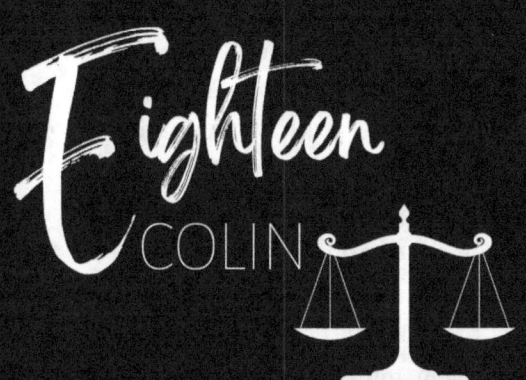

"Daphne, you in here?" I poke my head into her room, confused when I don't find her in bed. She wasn't in the kitchen or living room when I got back to the house a few minutes ago, and I can't imagine anywhere else she would be.

While Daphne was at work today, the girls and I went to see Scott and Ruth—Tabitha's parents. I'm confident in my decision to start dating again, in being with Daphne, but I still wanted their approval. Over an early dinner, we all shared stories of Tabitha—the girls chiming in with memories of their mom, before I grew enough of a pair to breach the subject of dating again.

Expecting to be met with apprehension, I was pleasantly surprised when not only did they both seem genuinely happy for me, but excited, too. They asked questions about Daphne, gushed over selfies and pictures of her with the girls that I hadn't seen before, and laughed as Emily and Laurel talked about the countless adventures they had been part of thanks to Daphne. After dinner, Ruth hugged me tight, tears in her eyes as she told me that it was good to see me smiling again, that it was good to see *me* again.

It seems like everyone in my life has been saying some version of the same thing lately.

Now, with the girls spending the night with Scott and Ruth, I'm thrumming with energy, anxious to spend some quality time with my girl.

Her voice calls out from across the room, behind the closed door of her en-suite bathroom. "In here!"

Placing the black bag that has been in the trunk of my car for the last two days on her bed, I cross to the bathroom door. Second guessing myself for only a split-second, I open the door without asking for permission, and steam comes wafting out of the bathroom. Daphne is submerged in water, next to none of her skin visible under the overwhelming amount of bubbles enveloping both the tub and her. I can't help but chuckle, her small face the only thing I can make out under the mountain of soapy bubbles. "What are you doing in there, Little Star?"

Melting further into the water, she lets out a sigh while pushing out her bottom lip in an adorable, exaggerated pout. "Just de-stressing a little bit after yesterday. I expected everything to go well, but still, the buildup was stressful. I couldn't help but keep thinking that there was a small part of your mom or the girls that would have thought I wasn't good enough for you."

Leaning over the side of the tub, I kiss her softly, not even caring that I'm getting vanilla scented bubbles all over myself. I love when she is vulnerable with me, when she shows me her beautiful emotions. "You, beautiful girl, are more than good enough. You're perfect—and perfect for me. Now, want to do something special for me?"

The bottom lip that was previously in a pout is now

captured between her teeth. "I always want to do something special for you."

I run my hand over her cheek before pushing myself up to stand. "There is a present for you on your bed." Daphne's eyes go wide, but I keep talking, not letting her speak. "If you're a good girl and finish up your bath, you can see what it is."

"Can I at least have a hint?"

Already at the door, I turn back to look at her beautiful smile. "Come upstairs and find me when you're done." Moving to close the door, I stop an inch short. "And Daphne?"

She looks to the door from where she is still submerged in the tub. "Yeah?"

"It's just Daddy and his Little Girl tonight."

I hear sloshing water before I hear the stopper being pulled from the drain, the telltale sound of water leaving the tub before the door even shuts that last inch, and I can't help the low rumble of laughter as I exit her room.

Tonight, I want to show her just how perfect she truly is.

When the knock comes on my bedroom door a short time later, I find myself equal parts anxious and excited. I wonder if she'll be wearing her gift, if she'll like what else I have for her. Thoughts of not being enough for her swirl through my own brain, and I take a fortifying sip of the whiskey I brought up to my room before pushing the thoughts from my head and calling out for her to enter.

Possibly the most perfect thing I have ever seen, she takes my breath away as she stands in the doorway for a moment before taking a tentative step inside. Daphne sweeps the room with her blue eyes, landing on me where I am seated in an over-sized, brown leather armchair.

The woman's body is made for sin, and just as I thought, the outfit I picked out for her on a whim is pure seduction. Sheer, white, thigh-high stockings cover her slim legs, a gentle band of lace around the top of each to hold it in place. Daphne wears a pale, pink skirt made of layers of ruffles, short enough that if she were to turn around, I would surely be able to see if she chose to wear panties. I'm torn between hoping she did so I can tear them from her body with my teeth and wanting her to have foregone them, so nothing stands between me and her perfectly-waxed pussy.

She turns me into an animal, and more and more, I find I like it.

"Come here," I manage to rasp out, entranced by the sight of her in my room, my domain, for the very first time.

Following my command, she crosses to where I stand, her nipples hard against the thin fabric of her matching pink crop top. The shirt dips low between her breasts, tying into a bow while delicate ruffles cover her shoulders. Sweet and sexy at the same time, just like the woman in front of me. "You like it?"

"I love it," she responds, all breathy.

From the arm of the chair, I take a long, thin jewelry box in my hand. "Can you get on your knees for me, baby? I've got one more gift for you."

Without hesitation, she drops to her knees, giving me her submission. It makes me feel powerful in a way I've never felt before, and if I wasn't already rock hard, the sight of her on her knees for me, staring up at my face through sweepingly long, black lashes, would have surely done it.

"I wanted to get something special for my Little Girl," I tell her. "But this is a present that we can only use when it's our extra special playtime. Does that sound like a rule you can follow?"

Daphne doesn't even know what is inside the box, but her body language gives away her excitement as she nods, almost vibrating in anticipation. Blue eyes with large, dilated pupils sparkle while her chest rises and falls, almost as if she's exerted herself after a hard workout.

Opening the small box for her, I present her with the second half of her gift. A thin, black choker rests against the black velvet. Silver letters line the choker, the words *Daddy's Girl* spelled out across the leather. Petite fingers reach out to trace over the letters. "Oh, Colin, it's beautiful."

"Colin?" I ask with a raised eyebrow and a stern tone.

Sheepishly, she looks away, acting every bit the little girl about to be in trouble for misspeaking. "I mean, Daddy. It's beautiful, Daddy."

I smile, proud of myself for getting this right. "Turn around, Little Girl. Let me put it on for you."

She obliges my request, turning around while still on her knees to face away from me. Daphne shivers when my fingers graze her skin, brushing her hair away from her neck. Gently, I remove the choker from the box, sliding it around her long, slim neck. Fastening the silver buckle, I then point to the full-length mirror across the room where our reflections dance together as one.

"Look how perfect you look, sitting between your Daddy's legs." Reaching out, I comb my fingers through her hair before working her long locks into two braids while Daphne sits, almost mesmerized by the movements of my fingers as I weave the plaits through the silky strands. Being an involved father to two daughters has taught me well when it comes to all sorts of fancy braids and twists.

It's dark outside, and the only light coming from within my room is from the small, antique lamp that sits on my nightstand. Still, even in the low lighting, I can see how beautiful she is as I study her while she continues to study us in the reflection.

We're a stark contradiction of one another almost all the time, but right now, with her kneeling at my feet in this wet dream of an outfit while I don black slacks and a white dress shirt, we couldn't look more different.

It's her soft, feminine body and my masculine edges. Her submission to the natural dominant side I never knew I had.

Leaning forward, I press a kiss to the exposed skin of her shoulder, watching as her eyes flutter closed. "Open your pretty, blue eyes, Little Girl. Keep your eyes on us."

Only when her eyes are finally open and fixed on the mirror do I guide her to her feet before pulling her into my lap, where her back melts to my chest, one leg splayed on either side of my thighs. All it would take is one small movement on my part to see if she's wearing panties, still I don't shift her just yet.

"Tell me what you see."

Daphne's voice is shaky when she speaks, and I'm unsure if it is from anticipation, anxiety, or a combination of the two. "I... I see myself in a beautiful outfit with a gorgeous collar. I see a strong, sexy Daddy behind me." I reach to the small table beside the chair, taking a sip of my whiskey, giving her time to continue. "I see your pretty, little girl who follows the rules and always does as her Daddy says. The little girl who likes to be dressed up as Daddy's little doll."

Dipping two fingers into the crystal glass, I bring them to her lips. "Suck, baby. Show your Daddy what you can do with that mouth."

Daphne's lips part slowly before she captures my fingers between them, savoring the flavor of the amber liquid. Her tongue flicks out over the digits before her teeth gently graze me.

"Will you tell me what you see, Daddy?"

Never a big talker during sex in the past, I find that it comes easy with Daphne, with my Little Girl. "Mmhmm. You might see a good girl, but I see a naughty princess who likes to tease her Daddy." Sliding one hand up her flat stomach, I take one end of the bow between her breasts while bringing my glass back to my lips with the other. "A very naughty girl who knows exactly what effect she has on me." I thrust under her, just once, but her soft moan tells me she feels exactly what she's capable of.

The fingers around the bow tug, opening to expose her breasts. Whiskey glass still in the other hand, I run the cool crystal over her nipples, the condensation from the glass dripping onto her hot skin. Her head lolls back against me, a low moan spilling from her lips, but the entire time, her eyes stay open.

"If you want something, you've got to use your words, Daphne." I let a few more drops of water drip down between her breasts, watching with rapt attention as they race down the flat plane of her stomach before soaking into the waistband of her skirt. "Unless you just want me to tease you all night."

She shakes her head. "No."

Tipping the glass over her torso, I let just the smallest amount of whiskey fall. With my other hand, I rub the liquid over her skin, taking my time to roll her nipples between my fingers before bringing them to her lips again.

Submissive little supplicant that she is, her lips part for me, allowing me to dip my thumb into her mouth before dragging it over the bottom lip I want so badly to bite.

Daphne begins to move back and forth over my lap, desperately seeking friction for what I can only imagine is a drenched pussy. But I don't let her get far, unsatisfied with her previous response. One of my arms snakes around her body, holding her still against my body. "You're going to have to do better than that, Little Girl."

She harrumphs, and while it's an insolent, bratty move, I love the way it sounds. "No, I don't want you to just tease me all day. I want to feel your hands on more of my body. I want your tongue on me and in me before you slide your cock deep inside me. I want every inch of my Daddy, and I want him to show me just how much he needs me."

I'm so hard that I'm about to burst out of my slacks as her dirty words sink in. "Using your words and making Daddy proud. Can you do one last thing for your Daddy before I give you all of what you want?"

This time, she full-on whines, earning herself a quick pinch of her nipple. "Keep up that attitude, and I won't let you come tonight."

"That's just mean!" It's still a whine and this time, instead of giving her a pass, I push to see just how far she'll go.

"Want to say that again to me, Little Girl?"

She seems to weigh her options for a few seconds, internally fighting with the angel and devil sitting on her shoulders, while she decides which path to traverse.

In the end, as to be expected with Daphne, the sassy sprite chooses violence.

"I said you're being a mean Daddy."

Without hesitation, I pick her up and set her on her feet. Shirt still hanging open, her upper half is on display to me via our reflection, and I decide at this moment that she should never wear a shirt again, those tight, rosy nipples too pretty to not be on display for me at all times.

"Face the mirror and get on all fours, Daphne. Your Daddy is about to punish you for your behavior."

And like the good girl that's hiding deep inside her right now, she does exactly as asked, wanting desperately to please me.

Nineteen

DAPHNE

Colin's gaze is liquid heat as he watches me drop to my knees before moving into position on all fours. I have no idea what his endgame is but watching every move we've made in the mirror in front of us has to be one of the most erotic things I've ever witnessed in my life.

Like, so hot that I'm confident I left a wet spot somewhere on Colin's slacks.

Whoopsies.

I was already relaxed from an extra-long bubble bath, and that relaxation quickly turned to desire when I saw the contents of the small, black bag that was waiting for me on my bed. The desire shifed to pure need when he presented me with my very own beautiful collar. I only wish I could wear it every day—could wear it as we walk down a sidewalk together, the entire world knowing that I'm his Little Girl.

Now, as I watch him wander the length of my body with his eyes, that need has turned to downright molten lava coursing through my entire system. Colin is content to get his fill, not in any hurry to touch me, all the while I continue to kneel on all fours, body burning from the inside out.

That backroad gravel is back in his voice when he speaks—a sound I first heard weeks ago, a sound that I now know means he's close to losing control. "I've been slowly dying tonight. Waiting to see if your cunt was going to be on display for me, and now that I know it is, I can't wait to taste it. But before I can do that, I'm going to have to spank that little ass of yours for backtalking and sassing me."

Spellbound, I watch as he rolls the sleeves of his dress shirt, watching as those delicious forearms come into view.

Seriously, forearm porn is a real thing, and Colin has it down to a fucking art.

Colin refills his glass from the crystal decanter atop a small table before he walks around my body, standing directly in front of me and blocking my view of our reflection. Crouching next to me, glass dangling from his fingers, he runs his free hand over my face, and I nuzzle into the smallest form of contact he's granted me. "Why does Daddy have to punish you, baby?"

"Because I was sassy, and Daddy doesn't accept smart mouths."

"That's right." He takes a sip from his glass before offering it to me, tipping it to allow the whiskey to flow into my mouth. It burns as I drink it down, furthering the heat that blooms within. As he pulls the glass away, some of the liquid trickles down my chin, and he wipes it away before sucking his thumb into his mouth.

Changing positions, he comes to kneel behind me. Grazing the hem of the skirt, he flips it up and over my ass before his palm firmly connects with my backside.

There is no warning, no gentle warmup over layers of clothes and panties, just his hand against my bare skin over and over. It's a shock to my senses, yet I find myself rocking back to meet him, wanting to feel it again and again and again.

His hand is heavy against my skin, and as the pain builds with each thwack, so does the sensation between my legs.

Alternating between staying in one spot and moving around, light and heavier movements, he delivers spank after spank, covering my ass until I'm confident he's turned me a nice rosy shade of red.

I watch, enthralled by our reflection in the mirror. The look of concentration of Colin's face, the way his eyes flare with each connection of our skin. The way I'm disheveled, breasts and ass and pussy on full display as he kneels behind me still fully dressed with a crystal tumbler dangling from his fingers.

Sure, I've had spankings before. Have been punished for having a dirty mouth and sassy attitude. But this...with Colin... isn't just a spanking. This is damn near as close to a religious experience as I've ever had.

Lead me to the altar, and I'll hands down be the first to convert.

Several smacks hit my sit spots, the tender flesh where my thighs and butt meet—a combination of a yelp and moan coming from me as they do. It's like he's determined to make me feel his hand long after our punishment is complete, and the thought wildly turns me on.

He's not tentative or meek, instead meeting each connection of our skin with a skilled hand. If I had to guess, he has been studying this, wanting to make sure I'm safe while still giving me what I desire. It's wildly attractive, how attentive he is, how eager he is to learn and lean into his new role.

After a few minutes of near constant impact, Colin begins to massage the globes of my ass, gentle caresses and touches that ease the stinging pain. "You know I never want to hurt you, Little Star. But you and I agreed on rules, and when you don't follow those rules, you need to be reminded that I'm in charge, that I always have your best interest at hand. Tell me, was I too hard on my Little Girl?"

God, he's so good at this—all stern yet gentle, and he doesn't even know it.

I give my sore butt a little wiggle while lowering my chest to the ground, wanting him to see the arousal that has grown between my thighs. "I know, Daddy. You only want what's best for me. You weren't too hard, you were perfect. You *are* perfect."

"That's right. You're such a smart girl, and you took your punishment so well." He says the words with a mixture of awe and reverence, making me feel cherished. And while all his words make me feel that way, they always hit a little deeper in moments of intimacy like the one we are currently sharing.

"Does that mean that I get to come tonight?"

Colin doesn't respond with words. Instead, he uses his hands, grazing his fingers up and down my back, over my ass and thighs. He uses his lips, pressing both open and closed mouth kisses over my skin. And he uses his tongue, taunting and teasing me with slow licks before finally...fucking *finally*...sliding his tongue over my cunt.

There is this cliché in romance novels that almost everyone makes fun of. That moment where the main character claims they let out a breath they didn't know they were holding. But I swear that after the over stimulation to every part of my body but where I most want it, when his tongue flicks out to taste me, I finally exhale a long-held breath—a romance novel cliché come to life.

"I'll never get over how good you taste," he rasps out against my skin. "So fucking sweet and so damn wet for me."

One of his large hands wraps around my hip, holding me in place. Expecting him to repeat the process on my other side, I squeak in surprise when instead, liquid hits me, running between my cheeks before trickling down between my lips.

Before it has a chance to travel further, Colin's mouth is back on me, lapping and licking at the combination of my arousal and his whiskey. I melt further into the floor beneath me, the coolness of the hardwood creating an exquisite contrast to the heat of my body. "Colin! Fuck!"

The words don't even finish leaving my mouth, and he's pulled away, one sharp slap landing on the sensitive flesh right between my legs. "I thought we talked about that dirty mouth of yours?"

In the mirror, I watch him stand and round my body, stopping in front of me. Fingers make quick work of his pants before pushing them down around his muscular thighs. Colin's cock juts forward, the thick head tapering to an equally as mouth-watering shaft. He's long and veiny, and my tongue darts out, desperate for a taste of him.

As if reading my mind, he commands me to kneel before fully divesting me of the top still loosely hanging from my body. "Mouth open, Little Girl. It seems as if the only way to make sure you behave is to put something in your mouth so you can't keep speaking."

I happily oblige, holding my mouth open wide while sticking out my tongue as if in an offering. Colin wastes no time, sliding himself deep inside, and on instinct, I wrap my lips around him. Over and over, he pumps himself into my mouth before pulling almost all the way out. Through my lashes, I watch as he holds himself on my tongue, pouring the remainder of liquid from his glass over his cock. Whiskey trails over his length in smooth rivulets before pooling on my tongue, and when my mouth is almost spilling over, he pulls his cock away. "Swallow," he commands, stroking my neck as the liquid travels down my throat to settle deep in my stomach.

He keeps his hand in place, our eyes locked in an epic battle of wills where neither of us wants to look away. Among the fire and electricity zapping between us, something shifts deep inside my soul.

Tonight, I don't want to be his little girl.

Tonight, I want to be the woman he adores.

Tonight, I want to be the woman he *loves*.

Because there isn't a doubt in my mind that I love Colin. And despite the fact that we've grown so close, that he has flourished in our time together, I know that he may never be able to say the same about me.

"Colin." It's a whispered plea, almost inaudible despite the silent room.

As if he's detected the change in me, his hand drops from my neck before he pulls me to my feet with ease. Wrapping his arms around me, he keeps me pressed against his solid chest, his hands smoothing up and down my spine in unhurried strokes. He unclasps the collar that has been around my neck, letting it fall to the ground.

Colin moves to my skirt, sliding it over my hips until it pools on the floor beneath me. My hand in his, he leads me to the bed, instructing me to sit atop the mattress while he kicks off his pants and unbuttons his shirt just enough to slip it over his head.

I fall back against the sheets when he begins to crawl over my body, holding himself up to look into my eyes. Colin presses his lips to the corner of my mouth in a sweet, chaste kiss as he positions himself between my legs.

The only man I've ever been with without protection slides into me, and I feast on the feeling of him inside of me with no barrier between us. Every inch, every glorious vein that lines his cock slides along my walls as he thrusts slowly again and again.

Dropping his forehead to mine, we share breaths before we share our lips with one another in a flurry of gentle kisses. There is nothing urgent about it, nothing frenzied or panicked.

Colin drops his head into the crook of my neck as if hiding away from me, and everything in my mind clicks into place.

It's why he took to the role of Daddy so easily, why he can be dominant and dirty. Because deep down inside, it's been the only way he felt he could be with me without truly feeling like he was doing something wrong. What we're doing now, the gentle kissing and caressing—it's not a role he's playing. It's him making love to me, telling me to hold on without words.

To just give him a little more time.

And for this man, for Colin, I would be willing to wait for my last breath because I know that when he loves, he loves with his entire heart.

Tonight, his actions are enough.

He sits up, pulling me with him while still fully seated inside of me. We rut together, our hips meeting, the sound of skin slapping together and echoing along with the sounds of our labored breathing.

"Daphne!" he rasps my name, almost a sob.

I cup his face in my hands, forcing him to look at me, forcing him to *see* me. I don't realize that I'm crying until the tears fall to our skin. My tears fall for him, for the love he had and lost. They fall for myself for the loss of the childhood I never got to have. They fall for the love and gratitude I have for this man in front of me, for the past we've both navigated alone and the future I pray he wants to navigate together. "I know," I gasp out around sobs as our bodies continue to move together.

His lips press against mine in a searing kiss. A combination of the taste of my own arousal on his lips mix with the salt of my tears, and through the emotions and damages we share, the coming together of our bodies and our minds, I decide it is my new favorite flavor. More of the words he can't yet say, more silent promises. It's a beautiful display of adoration and love. His eyes are misty, much like my own, yet despite the emotion we're both feeling, we tumble closer to the edge together.

"I need you," he says as one hand tangles in my hair. "So fucking bad."

I nod, feeling the same. *Needing* the same. "I'm yours, Colin. Take what you need—I'm *yours.*"

As if he needed my permission, he thrusts a few more times before exploding inside me.

"Fuck," he yells before reaching down to rub circles on my clit while he continues to pulse inside me. "Come, Daphne."

And I do.

My walls clench down on him, pulling the last of his own orgasm from his body. My back stiffens and my breath catches as my body fills with the sensation of white-noise static on an old-school television set.

Colin holds me in his arms, hugging me through the aftershocks that roll through my body before gently guiding me to the mattress. His cum leaks from between my legs, but when he pulls my body to his, spooning me against his nakedness, all thoughts of cleaning up disappear from my brain.

We don't talk, just lazily lay together. I'm not sure which one of us dozes off first, but when I wake in the middle of the night, the body of a giant wrapped around my own, I know without certainty that I'm home and that I've finally found my family.

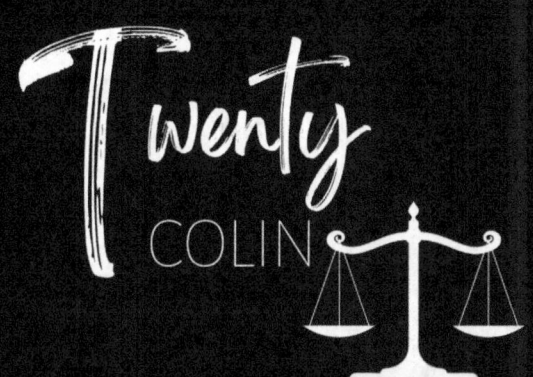

Twenty
COLIN

A GENTLE BREEZE WINDS ITS WAY THROUGH THE TREES, much in the same way I'm winding my way through the cemetery toward the final resting place of my wife. My feet move on their own accord, almost as if my body turns on autopilot the moment I drive through the wrought-iron gates.

Coming to rest beside her headstone, I lower myself to my knees, swiping away the layers of dirt and leaves that threaten to cover the last remnants of her life here on earth. A simple life represented by the small, almost insignificant dash between two dates.

At first, I used to come to visit Tabitha almost weekly. Over time, those visits turned bi-weekly, before turning monthly, before turning into just once in the last six months. I'm not sure why I've been putting it off, maybe afraid that the grief I've felt for so long will continue to plague me or that suddenly, that grief won't feel as overwhelming, making me feel as if I've forgotten her.

Forgotten the us that once was.

Fully sitting in the long, brown fall grass, I place the bouquet of pink carnations against the stone where her name is engraved. She loved these silly flowers, the cheaper the better, and swore they lasted twice as long as any bouquet of roses ever would. As with everything she believed, she was right. The thought makes me smile, thinking back to all the times I stopped at the corner store on my way home from the office to pick up a fresh bouquet for her, knowing she loved fresh flowers in the house.

I don't bother to look around for privacy, unafraid of the tears that well up in my eyes while I share this sacred time with her.

"I'm sorry it's been so long since I've been here, Tabby Cat," I speak to the air, the ghosts of the past swirling around me, almost making music of the wind as it whips around. "I miss you so goddamn much it hurts. We all do—the girls, my mom, your parents and brother."

Reaching out, I swirl my hand over the words etched across her headstone—mother, wife, daughter, sister. "The girls are great, so great. They're growing so fast. Laurel's in college now. She's interested in boys and shopping. And Emily," I sigh, "well, she's exactly like you. Caring and kind. Gentle and nurturing.

"Last week, a bird flew into the side of the house, and you know our girl picked that weak, stunned, little birdie up without hesitation, begging me to help her save it. Which, of course, I did. You know I can't say no to anything they ever ask of me. Just like I could never say no to you."

I pause, drawing in a deep breath, my tears freely flowing. Running my finger over my ring, I look up to the sky, almost as if willing her to appear here by my side, if even just for a small moment in time.

"It's just, hard, you know—doing this on my own. We were

such a good team, Tabs. The best damn team. I know if you were here, you'd laugh at me and point out that I have my mom, Mina, and Nico. That I still have your parents and can always call your brother. But some days, it's just not enough. We were supposed to be together forever. We were supposed to grow old together and spend our weekends sitting on the back porch, passing the Sunday crossword puzzle back and forth while sipping on hot coffee. We were supposed to travel and explore the world together after the girls left for college, and dammit if I don't feel cheated out of having all of those experiences with you."

Brushing the tears away from my face, I inhale deeply before continuing.

"And if you can believe it, at the same time that I've been sitting here over the last two and a half years, the same time I've been feeling cheated because of everything we missed, I managed to meet someone." The tears really come now, cascading down my cheeks and falling on the fabric of my t-shirt where they dampen the gray cotton.

"She's not you, Tabs. No one ever will be. Still, I think you would like her. Believe it or not, she's my sister's best friend."

I can't help but laugh out loud, knowing the exact look Tabitha would give me if she were beside me right now, her eyes widened in shock.

"I wish you could see her with the girls. See how she has been there for them since the very moment she met them. From homework to talking about boys and everything from fashion to making sure they are well fed when I have to be at work late—she's done it all without ever batting an eye. She's simply stepped into this role of a mentor to the girls next to me as their father. It wasn't something I ever intended or asked of her, but she has done it all without any thought of herself or her future.

She truly wants the best for our girls, and it makes my heart ache and bloom at the same time.

"All the while, at the same time she's been creating this awesome, selfless bond with them, she's been doing the same with me. And it makes me feel so guilty, Tabby Cat. It makes me feel like I'm pushing your memory aside. And even though the girls approve, I worry they will begin to think that I am trying to replace you, which we both know could never happen. Still, it almost paralyzes me with fear at times. Other times, I'll catch myself laughing with her late into the night about absolutely nothing yet absolutely everything all at the same time."

My lips quirk up, thinking of last week when Daphne turned around to walk back to her bedroom after a particularly steamy, late-night kitchen hookup and slipped in a puddle of Stella's pee in the hallway. Poor old thing—Stella, not Daphne —can barely hold it in anymore. Daphne hit the ground with a thud, and after a moment of stunned silence, she simply burst into laughter. I couldn't help but follow in her footsteps, both of us laughing so loudly that we woke Emily. We ended up making up some excuse about a late-night plumbing issue on the spot as the reason we were both in the kitchen in our pajamas in the middle of the night, not trying to raise any suspicion with the teenager who is too smart for her own good.

"She's the exact opposite of you, yet she has so many of the same qualities you possessed. So many of the same qualities you instilled in our girls that sometimes, it's almost scary.

"I know you, Tabs, you're up there right now, telling me to get to the point. To stop babbling and just say what's on my mind. Isn't it funny that I've always been able to do that with everyone but you? I can command a courtroom full of people, talk to my mom or two teenagers with no problem, but having to say something hard to you...to say this to you..."

Sliding off my ring, I grasp it tightly in my fist, feeling the metal as it digs into my skin. Tilting my chin to the sky, I tightly shut my eyes, my lips quivering.

"I love her, Tabitha. God knows it will never come close to the love I have for you, for the love that we shared, but I love her, and I don't want to feel guilty about it anymore. I will forever keep your memory alive for our daughters, forever keep our memories alive for myself, but I am giving myself permission to move on, and I'm sorry if that hurts you. I never want to hurt you.

"In time, I hope you can come to accept her in our lives, and I pray you know this isn't me turning my back on you or what we shared while you were on Earth. But I need this, Tabs. She gives me hope. She makes me feel alive, painting the world with colors as rich and vibrant as she is, and that's a feeling I haven't had since you were taken from me. I love her. But the love I hold in my heart for her will never replace the love I hold in my heart for you. I love you baby, so much.

"This isn't because I don't love you anymore. This isn't because I've stopped caring for you or the life we had together. This isn't me being selfish or unkind. It's simply me knowing now that I can grieve for you and love you while loving her at the same time. This was like a life raft for me." I squeeze my fist tighter around the ring. "I was so afraid to take it off, of what that would symbolize to our daughters, to our families, to the world. But I'm not afraid of that anymore, baby. Because I know that I can keep you in my heart for the rest of my life while loving another. That I can love and cherish our time together while working on a future with Daphne. That deep down, you would want this for me. Would want me to feel this strange sensation in my chest that can only be described as happiness. In fact, if I know you even an ounce as well as I think I do, I wouldn't be surprised if somehow, you've been behind the scenes all along, helping to push me toward the perfect person for me. The perfect person to help raise our daughters. The perfect person to hold my heart."

Opening my eyes, I crouch until I'm directly in front of the headstone. I drop my forehead to the cool stone, allowing a few tears to fall on the earth beneath my feet, my chest vibrating with emotion.. Pushing myself to my full height, I unclasp my hand, looking at my ring and the indent of its outline against the fleshy skin of my palm. Delicately picking it up with my right hand, I place it equally as delicately on top of her headstone, this time consciously rubbing my finger over the now bare space before walking away.

Twenty-One

DAPHNE

My day has been filled with back-to-back appointments—a large thigh piece full of intricate and ornate flowers, a gorgeous mandala on a first-timer's forearm, and a fine-line butterfly that looks like it's bursting out of an explosion of geometric shapes.

While I've always tried my hardest not to let my personal life interfere with my work, I've been feeling a little off lately and can definitely tell that my head has been in the clouds.

Halloween and Thanksgiving have come and gone, a coldness settling into the air around us, and as we creep closer and closer to Christmas, I've begun to feel that familiar cold in my bones, too.

It's normal for me to get this way around Christmas, around the anniversary of the day I lost the only family I knew until I was seven years old, but I can't help but feel that something else is bothering me, too. I'm just not sure what it is.

After finishing up with my last appointment of the night, I walk over to Mina, who is putting her own finishing touches on a gorgeous Neo-traditional style cat surrounded by small, blooming flowers. Watching as she blends colors until she is satisfied with the results is fascinating to me. Sure, I can crank out a decent color piece with the best of them, but the way Mina works in color is simply hypnotizing.

Looking up from her work, Mina points to a stack of papers sitting on her station. "Have you had a chance to look through any of the applicants yet?"

Since reopening after our remodel a few months ago, we've barely been able to keep up with the customer demand at the shop. While I would love to take on more hours, the added work has been wreaking havoc on my back and wrist. Hours bent over a table and repetitive motions will do that to anyone, but in our line of work, it isn't rare for people to end up with carpal tunnel, slipped discs, or worse. Instead of risking injury to myself or any of our artists, Mina and I have agreed that it is time to bring in at least one more full-time artist.

I take the stack of papers and thumb through the pages. "I haven't even had a chance to pee all day, let alone get through these. I'll take them to the office and start looking through them now."

Nodding, she promises to meet me in the office when she's done with her appointment.

Inside the office, I poor wine from our office mini-fridge into a plastic cup and then settle into the comfortable armchair in the corner with the stack of papers balanced on top of my knees.

One by one, I review each application, setting several to the side that stand out from the rest until only a dozen or so resumes remain.

My phone buzzes where it is perched on the arm of the chair, and I quickly answer it with a smile on my face when I see Colin's name on the screen.

"Hey," he says in a clipped tone. "I hate to bother you when you're at work."

Even though it is almost eight at night, it sounds like he isn't at home yet either. Instead, I hear the low chatter of voices in the background.

"You're never a bother, you know that."

Colin sighs, and he sounds exhausted, almost defeated. "I appreciate it. Anyway, I just wanted to let you know that some stuff came up at work. I'm still working, and I'm not sure what time I'll be home tonight."

Mina comes into the office, laughing at the various stacks of paper strewn around me. She takes the chair behind the desk while I continue my conversation with her brother. "Is Emily at the house alone? I was just going over a few resumes with Mina, but I can finish that up with her tomorrow if you need me to get home."

"No, my mom picked her up about an hour ago. She's going to stay at her condo for the night."

I shouldn't feel hurt that he sent Emily to stay with his mom for the night but knowing that I wasn't the first person he called stings a little.

"Oh," is my only response.

"So take your time getting home, and I'm sorry, but you'll probably want to grab dinner on your own."

If this is what lawyer Colin is like, I'm not a fan.

I always imagined that boardroom Colin would be the same as bedroom Colin, all passion and fire—minus the dirty mouth, of course. But this, the annoyed tone and quick responses don't make him seem powerful; they just make him seem annoyed.

We hang up after a brief goodbye, and I just stare at my phone for a few seconds before placing it back on the arm of the chair. Picking up the stack of papers I haven't gotten to yet, I look at my best friend. "Okay, let me just go through these quick, and we can narrow it down." I point to a pile on the edge of the desk. "That's the pile of people I've liked so far."

Mina pours herself a glass of wine then settles back into the chair, but she doesn't move to pick up the stack of papers. "What's going on, Daphne?"

I can't help the tears that well up in my eyes. "I don't know."

"Is it everything this time of the year reminds you of, or is my brother being an asshole?"

"Yes. No. I don't know."

She comes around the desk and sits on top of it, so she is in front of me. Cradling my hands in hers, Mina continues, "You can talk to me, babe. You know that. Unless it's sexual, then I don't want to hear a thing."

As always, she finds a way to make me smile, even when I'm feeling lower than low. "I'm really not sure. I expect to be sad at this time of the year, that's just something that happens whether I want it to or not. But it just feels like something else big is getting ready to happen. Things have been so good with your brother, especially since I moved into his room."

The previous week, after a wonderful night of making love and whispering secrets to each other early into the morning, Colin asked me if I would move into his suite upstairs with him. He told me he didn't want to spend another night in separate bedrooms, that he wanted me in his arms every night when he fell asleep, and that he wanted my face to be the first thing he saw each morning. I cried, overwhelmed at the love running through my body every time I looked at him. That night, I came home from work to find he had moved my belongings into his room, making space in the closet for my clothes and in the bathroom for my toiletries. My prized collection of paperbacks were neatly stacked on a bookshelf in the living room, and several of the cute collectibles I had purchased over the years had been integrated into the main living area of the house.

Only when we moved to go to bed did my eyes land on the framed photo of me and my mom that was placed on my nightstand. Wrapped in each other's arms, it's one of the few pictures I have of the two of us together, and I would no less than run into a burning building to save it. In the picture, my mom's hair cascades around us, our identical blue eyes staring back at the camera as we smiled. I don't remember where we were or what we were doing, but every time I look at that picture, it's like she is still here with me, frozen in time. I had it tucked loosely into the corner of the mirror in my room downstairs, and not only had Colin brought it upstairs into what is now our room, but he placed it in a frame, too.

Still holding my hands, Mina gives them a little squeeze, dragging me back to the office we're sitting in. "And then Colin was just really short on the phone with me. He said he was still at work, Emily was with his mom for the night, and that he didn't know when he'd be home. It just...it feels like the other shoe is going to drop at any minute, and it's making my stomach tie itself in freaking knots. What if he's decided he can't do it? That he wants me to move back downstairs, or even worse, out of the house?"

"Hey," Mina croons out softly. "Listen to me. First, shit happens in his profession and sometimes he has to handle things after hours. I'm sure he's just stressed with whatever is going on. And as far as him calling my mom, he's been on his own for so long, relied on her for so long, that it is only natural for him to default to calling her. Don't take that personally."

I get up and refill both of our glasses, feeling better but not fully convinced. Mina doesn't let up when she asks, "How many books have you read this year?"

"I'm not sure, probably somewhere around two-hundred."

"And how many of them were romance books?"

Grimacing, I look at my friend who is waiting with rapt attention. "I don't know, a hundred and fifty?"

"And I bet almost all of them have some dramatic third-act breakup where the main characters find themselves at odds with one another, one groveling to save the relationship when they realize they made some major mistake."

I give her a shrug. "I mean, yeah, it's kinda a major plot point for most of them."

"But babe, *that's* what I'm saying. That's *fiction*. I'm not here to discount the fact that they're amazing to read, but they aren't real. They're written for our entertainment. Maybe real life doesn't have some big third-act twist."

My phone beeps and I pick it up, swiping across the screen to read the message that just came from Colin. Sighing, my stomach sinking, I hold out the phone to my best friend. "If they don't happen in real life, then why did I just get this message?"

She reads the screen, looking back and forth between me and my now shaking hands before muttering, "Well, fuck."

In the open text message thread, his most recent message simply reads, *we need to talk.*

Twenty-Two

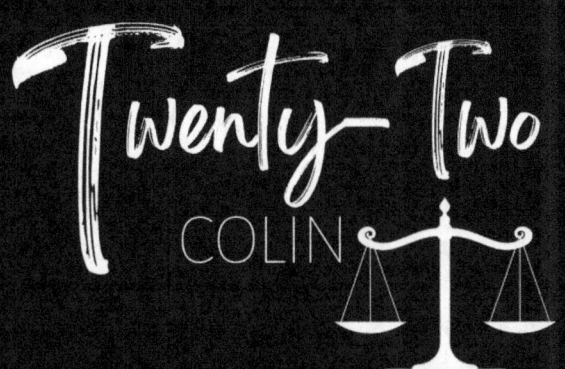

COLIN

I HEAR DAPHNE'S SUV AS IT PULLS UP OUTSIDE MY office. It's nearly ten at night, and while it isn't the latest I've ever been here, it's definitely cutting it close.

My office sits in an old, remodeled house that isn't that different from where we currently live. Though inside, the kitchen has been transformed into a conference room, the bedrooms upstairs are storage, and each of the lawyers that work here have their own office on the ground floor along with a receptionist station when you first enter.

Opening the door before she can knock, I pull Daphne into a hug the second she crosses the threshold. One hand fists her hair as I tilt my head to inhale her scent, still fresh after a long day at work. My eyes close, and I spend a solid minute just standing there with her in my arms.

She pulls away, looking askance. "Colin, what's going on? You're starting to worry me."

Letting out a sigh, I rub my hand over my face. "Come back to my office with me please."

I lock the front door, and Daphne follows me to my office. She sits in one of the two chairs across from my desk, and instead of walking around the desk to sit in my office chair, I sit next to her.

"Today..." I start, but I find it hard to continue, "Today fucking sucked, Daphne. I got a call from Child Protective Services. There was an incident with one of my clients."

At that moment, a tiny noise in the corner of the room draws Daphne's attention. She gasps when her eyes land on the car seat that's sitting on the ground in the corner of my office.

"Is that a baby?" she asks incredulously. "What is a baby doing in your office?

The tightly wrapped bundle squirms before calming down, but I still cross to the car seat and lift the little guy into my arms, swaddling him against my chest. "Daphne, I'm about to ask something of you, and I don't know if it is something you can commit to, but if I didn't ask, I'd never forgive myself."

Her eyes dart between me and the baby, back and forth, like she can't quite place what she is seeing.

"This is Joseph, and he is three days old. My contact with CPS is trying to locate something long-term, but in the meantime, he needs to be placed in emergency foster care. Tabitha and I had completed all the requirements a few years ago, so I was the first person the agent called.

"I know this is asking a lot of you. I know you don't particularly like kids, so I can't imagine you would be anymore keen on the idea of a baby in the house, even if just for a few days. But if you can do this for him, if you say yes, I'll handle everything. I'll take care of bottles and baths, diapers and middle-of-the-night feedings."

I plead with my eyes as she looks at me, unconvinced. I can see the trepidation all over her beautiful face, and I fear if I do the right thing by this tiny bundle in my arms that I'll lose her, lose the woman who brought me back to life.

Because that is exactly what Daphne did. She's not the woman who threw me a life raft when I was drowning. No, she's the woman who jumped right into the tumultuous water and treaded right alongside me, making it easier to survive with simply her presence by my side.

Her voice is hoarse when she finally breaks her silence. "Where are his parents?"

I bounce Joseph in my arms when he starts to fuss, probably ready for a bottle after his day. "I can't get into specifics."

"Colin, please. You have to give me something. This is a fucking huge decision. Shit," she stammers, her hands coming up to tug at the strands of her hair, "I shouldn't be cursing in front of a baby!"

As serious as the situation is, I can't help a small chuckle. "Little Star, I don't think he's quite that impressionable just yet."

She doesn't give me a sassy retort, just continues to look at the baby, almost as if she's never seen one before. "You can't tell me anything about why he is here? About how long he would be with us?"

"His father's parental rights are in the process of being terminated as we speak."

"What about his mother?"

I close my eyes for a second and when I reopen them, I stare at Daphne, giving her as much of the truth as I legally can. "She was murdered last night."

Her face visibly pales, a tormented look twisting her normally delicate features as her hands come up to cup her mouth. "Did...was it the father?"

Solemnly, I nod, and when I do, she shatters into a million pieces in front of me, sobbing uncontrollably. Quickly scanning my office, she runs to my wastebasket, vomiting until there is nothing left in her stomach to expel.

By the time I return Joseph to his car seat and get to her side, she's trembling, her entire body heaving with some emotion she has yet to share with me. I sit on the ground next to the trash can, not even caring about the stench emanating from the wastebasket, but simply needing to know that she's okay.

"Baby," I soothe as I pull her into my arms, "I've got you. It's too much. I knew it would be too much to ask right now with how new things are between us. I never expected to get this phone call, never even thought that it was a possibility. I'll call Cynthia back and have her move to the next person on her list."

Through hiccupping sobs, she manages to call out, "No! That's not it."

On the hideous antique rug that sits under my desk, I pull her closer, situating her on my lap. Rubbing circles on her back, I mimic the motions I saw my sister do to her all those months ago on the first day she moved into my house, the motions I just used to calm down the now sleeping baby boy in a car seat on my office floor. She's my beautiful, broken, little girl, and I want nothing but to take away any pain she ever feels, whatever it is. "Talk to me."

Daphne sucks in several large gulps of air, as if trying to fill her lungs after being held underwater to the verge of her breaking point. She wipes her hands over her tear-streaked face before burrowing her head into the crook of my neck. Her voice trembles as she talks, and I can tell she has to keep forcing herself to continue. "You know that next week is the anniversary of my mom's death—God, I miss her so much. But what you don't know, what barely anyone knows Colin, is that..." A sob escapes and I hug her closer, silently urging her to go on. "What barely anyone knows is that my dad killed her. He was a worthless piece of shit that killed her, and after he killed her, he put a bullet in his own head."

My poor, sweet girl. I want to take away her pain, want to erase this from her memory and replace it with nothing but sunshine and the best parts of our future together. But sadly, I'm still only a human, and all I can do is to be here for her.

"I'm so sorry, baby. So, damn sorry."

"That's the worst part," she says. "He killed her, and then he killed himself, and he never even had to pay for what he did to her. For what he did to *me*. He took away my mom, but he also took away my first best friend, my protector, the only person who ever kept me safe until I met you."

"God, what I wouldn't do to be able to take this pain from you."

Small tremors still work their way through her body as she calms down. Head still safely tucked into my neck, her hand comes up to rest on my chest. "It sucks...so fucking bad, but it's made me who I am. I miss my mom, and I will every day. But Colin, having that experience makes me confident when I tell you that Joseph is coming home with us tonight. He's not going somewhere else. I can't let that happen."

Never in a million years did I think this was how my conversation with Daphne was going to go tonight. If I'm being honest, I expected yelling, more than a few choice words, and a firm and absolute no.

And I would have been okay with that no, but I *had* to try. Hell, I wasn't exactly ready to have a newborn in the house again, but it was only going to be for a few days, and Joseph deserved safety and warmth, especially during the first days of his little life.

Pushing away from my body, she looks up at me, those big, blue eyes red-rimmed from her tears. "I'm in my mid-thirties, and I've never changed a diaper before."

"I told you, I'll take care of everything."

Daphne shakes her head. "No, I want to learn."

"Well, I guess it's a good thing that I'm kind of a pro. I mean, it's been a few years, but I bet I've still got it. I'll teach you my ways." I wave a hand in front of my face as if doing some slight-of-hand magic trick.

"The fuck are you? A Jedi master?" She playfully swats at me, some of the light returning to her always expressive eyes.

I give her a wink while laughing before pulling her into me once again, never wanting to let her leave my arms. "Nah, Little Girl, not a Jedi master. Just a Daddy who never wants to see his girl in pain."

Daphne smiles at me, not the beaming smile that shines through her entire body, but a small smile that shows me that she knows I have her best interest at heart.

For now, I'll take it.

We slowly rise from the floor, and I dispose of the garbage bag in the dumpster behind the house, while Daphne quickly freshens up in the bathroom.

When I come back into my office, she's crouched on the ground, staring at the bundle of blankets and the perfectly round little face looking back at her with big, brown eyes. I don't interrupt their moment, allowing them to slowly study each other, but I don't miss when she leans even closer, placing the gentlest of kisses upon his tiny forehead before whispering to him just barely loud enough for me to hear, "Don't worry, little Joseph. I'll keep you safe."

And Daphne has nothing to worry about either, because at the same time she is making that promise to baby Joseph, I'm silently making the same promise to her.

Twenty-Three

DAPHNE

When I was in high school, I was known as a party girl. I was hanging out with boys at the local community college, while girls my age were studying for their standardized tests, sneaking into bars and nightclubs when my peers were more concerned with sneaking into R-rated movies.

By the time I reached college, not much had changed. One time, at a particularly raucous campus party, the cops were called, and we all scattered. I woke up the next morning in the middle of a cornfield with no recollection of how I got there. Seriously, I blacked out somewhere in Iowa, and next thing I knew, I was in the middle of a field of corn somewhere across the border in Nebraska.

That was enough of a wakeup call for me to get my shit together, but that's beside the point.

The point is, that even with the hard partying ways of my teens and early twenties, along with the crazy and odd hours I've worked over the years, I have never...and I mean *never*, been as tired as I am right now.

Baby Joseph—or BJ for short—has been with us for almost two weeks. What started as emergency placement quickly turned into short-term placement when no other members of his mother's family stepped forward to take on the responsibilities of raising a newborn.

It's been one hell of a steep learning curve, harder than I ever thought possible. I've been peed on more times than I can count, have learned that babies can, in fact, shit so much that it leaks out of their diapers and onto the unsuspecting poor soul holding them in that moment—spoiler alert, that poor soul was me—and I haven't slept for more than four hours at a time since the night we brought him home.

I know Colin said he would take care of everything—the feedings, changings, and bathing, but I didn't want him to hold that responsibility alone.

We've created a little tag team, one of us always at home while the other works. Thankfully, with Colin having a home office, he has been able to be even more flexible with his schedule than normal, and while I used to spend a lot of time at Broken Sparrow creating designs for my upcoming appointments, I've shifted to doing that work at home, giving us even more time together.

I have baby vomit on my shirt, my hair hasn't been washed in four days, and I'm fairly confident the unwelcoming aroma I currently smell is wafting off of me.

Still, sitting here in the rocking chair we put in the pseudo nursery nook of the bedroom while BJ drinks from his bottle, his little mouth making the cutest little sucking noises—hell, I wouldn't trade it for the world.

Positioning him on my shoulder, I begin a routine of gently circling his back while working in several light pats. That's another thing I never would have guessed, but man is this little peanut gassy.

I quietly hum *Baby Mine* from *Dumbo* as we rock, a song I can still vividly remember my mom singing to me. It was always her favorite movie, and I guess she passed that love onto me in some small way.

Sensing Colin, I look up from Baby Joseph to find him standing in the bathroom doorway, simply observing us. Low-slung joggers sit on his hips, and while he's skipped a shirt after his shower, he is wearing those glasses he so rarely wears.

Those glasses do something to me.

Crossing the room, he bends down to take the baby from me, dropping a kiss on my lips as he does. "I never thought I'd see the day where I'd be even more attracted to you than I already was, but I have to say, standing there, watching you soothe this little guy—it takes my breath away, Daphne."

"Even with curdled milk formula vomit on my shirt?" I give him a little roll of my eyes as I stand from the rocker, ready for my own scheduled shower time.

He has the baby in his arm, snuggled up against his bare chest, yet he manages to grab me before I can walk past him, pulling me into his arms with Joseph nestled between us. It's intimate and beautiful, and somewhere deep within my body, my fallopian tubes flutter. At least, I think they would if they could.

"Yeah," he says evenly. "Even with curdled milk formula vomit on your shirt."

"You're insane, you know that?"

Colin beams down at me from where he stands so broad and tall. "Not insane, baby. Just insanely in love with you."

I gasp his name, gazing up into his green eyes, studying the small flecks of gold that radiate out, creating little sunbursts inside his irises.

He speaks quietly, not wanting to startle BJ, but regardless of his volume, his words almost bring me to my knees. "It's true.

I'm sorry it's not some grand gesture like in your books. I wanted to make it special, wanted to make it something you would remember for the rest of your life. But then seeing you there with him, listening to you hum to him and rub his sweet, little back. I just couldn't wait."

A few tears fall as I stare up into his eyes, but when I try to talk, he silences me.

"No, wait. I'm not done yet. Daphne, I love you. You're absolutely stunning, and you don't even know it. You're sassy as hell and madly infuriating at times, but I *love* that about you. You're everything my girls could have ever asked for in a bonus family member, a bonus *mother*. Because though you didn't ask for it, that's the role you've stepped into, and you did it so flawlessly and without even knowing. They may be Tabitha's biological daughters, but with your influence, you're going to be just as much as part of them as she ever was, and I'll be damned if that doesn't make me beam with pride."

Tears fall freely now, and yet Colin keeps talking, looking at me with such reverence that it makes time stand still around us. "I thought I lost it all when I lost Tabitha, and there will always be a part of me missing, but now I know that I needed that experience with her, I needed her love and the loss that came with it. Because that love and loss brought me to you, and I can't imagine a day without you in my life. I can't do everything alone, but with you by my side, I can do anything, Daphne. Fucking *anything*. And yes, I just cursed in front of the baby, and I'll put a dollar in the swear jar, but that's how much I mean it."

I laugh loudly, and Baby Joseph flinches in response, but I can't even help it. I made the swear jar as a joke and told Colin and Emily to make me put a dollar in it every time I cursed in front of the baby and that when he went to his forever family, that it would be the start of his college fund. Swear to God, the thing already has like a hundred bucks in it.

"I know I told you I wanted all your mornings and nights a few weeks ago when you moved into my room, but damnit, I want all the in-betweens too. I want to celebrate every one of your successes with you, and I want to be there to take the sting out of your disappointments. Tell me that you want that too. Tell me that you love me Daphne, that you'll spend forever with me."

"Of course I fucking love you!" I almost yell it into the space, even though he is just a few inches away from me. "I lusted after you for so long, a crush I harbored from afar. But God, it's so much more than that now, Colin. You're everything I've ever wanted, more than I ever could have dreamed of. I love you, I love you, I love you!"

He beams down at me, a stunning smile of straight, white teeth, and while I've seen Colin smile more and more over the last few months, nothing beats the way he's smiling at me right now.

Our lips meet with an infant still cradled between our bodies. "Forever, Daphne. Spend forever with me?"

"Are you...are you asking what I think you're asking? Because if you're not, this is one hell of a mean prank."

His laugh is infectious. "See, sassy and infuriating, even when I'm asking you to marry me."

I grin back at him. "It's a good thing you're holding BJ right now, or I'd seriously consider tackling you. My answer is forever a yes, Colin. I told you all those months ago, I was yours in whatever way you could give yourself to me. But this, this is beyond words."

"I know you did, baby. And I never doubted it, never doubted *you*. But how many times do I have to tell you, his name is Joseph."

"BJ for short. How many times have I told *you* this? Emily and I agreed on it."

"Daphne, people are going to make fun of him! You don't name a kid BJ!" He whisper shouts at me, like he doesn't want the baby to hear our discussion.

I fall into a fit of giggles again as he pushes me away. "Go shower that curdled milk formula vomit smell off your body. Then we're going to buy the biggest diamond I can find to put on that ring finger of yours before everyone comes over for dinner tonight. I want everyone to know that you're mine."

"Damn, ask for my hand in marriage, and you go all caveman on me! I like this side of you."

A salacious grin spreads across his face. "Just wait till everyone is gone tonight and this little one goes to sleep. You want caveman? Well hold on, Little Star, cause Daddy is about to go primal."

I walk from the room laughing and shaking my head in disbelief.

I have the best friend a girl could ever ask for, the most amazing man by my side, and a family that's growing at every turn.

Oh, and did I mention that I'm engaged to the man of my dreams?

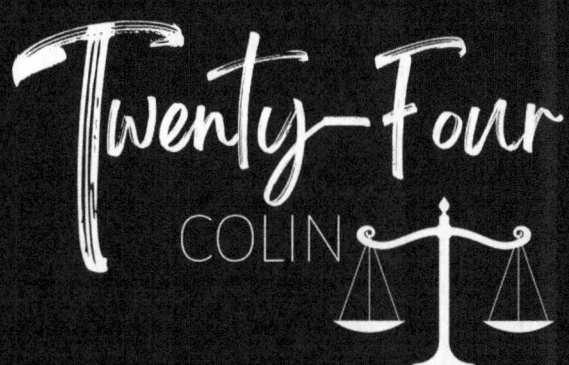

Twenty-Four
COLIN

AT THIS TIME LAST YEAR, IF YOU'D HAVE TOLD ME I would be engaged to my sister's best friend, I probably would have laughed in your face. Actually, not even probably. I definitely would have laughed in your face.

Yet here I am tonight, laying in bed with the woman I never knew I needed until she was thrust upon my life. We're both naked, except for the giant diamond glinting in the moonlight. Daphne tried to talk me out of it when we saw the price tag, but I saw the way her face lit up when I slid that particular ring on her finger, and much like the two teenagers who own me, I can't say no to Daphne either.

Not that I wanted to say no. Even if she refused, I would have just gone back to the jeweler tomorrow and bought it anyway. When it just so happened to fit her perfectly, I told her it was meant to be as she beamed up at me with tears in her eyes.

I had tears in my eyes, too.

When everyone sat in the dining room for dinner tonight, we kept quiet, going about our night like normal. We were halfway through our meal when my mom jumped up from the table, knocking her chair onto the ground in one swift movement while running around the table to all but tackle my fiancée.

God, that feels great to say.

After everyone else at the table caught on to what was happening, hugs and congratulations were passed all around with more than just a few tears of happiness shed as well. We toasted with a bottle of champagne—a Christmas present from a client—while Baby Joseph slept peacefully nearby in his swing. Even the girls, Laurel being home on winter break, were able to celebrate with us, and they both indulged in sparkling cider while giving me and Daphne extra-long hugs.

And this time, Laurel and Nico split the pot.

Because naturally, they were still betting on things when it came to me and Daphne.

Now with the girls at their friends' houses for the night, it's just me and Daphne in the quiet of the house, while Joseph sleeps in his crib nearby. It's only a little after ten, but we've been in bed since just after seven, my mom offering to take on full dish duty so we could get a little bit of much needed rest.

"Is this what being a parent is always like?" Daphne asks me while drawing slow, lazy circles over my chest with her blue fingernails.

"Utterly exhausting but equally as rewarding? Yeah, it is." Capturing her hand with mine, I study the ring on her finger before placing a kiss to her palm.

She gives me a little smile, looking up at me through her impossibly long lashes. "I never thought I'd like it."

"You once told me I was a natural at being a Daddy. While

in an entirely different sense of the word, you're a natural at being a mother. It's in the way you love with every fiber of your being. It's inspiring to watch."

"How did I get lucky enough to find you?" she asks me with raw, quaking vulnerability in her voice.

"I ask myself the same thing about you every day."

Joseph starts to fuss in his crib, and Daphne starts to move. "Let me take care of him. Want to go downstairs and get us some dessert to share? I'll come down as soon as I get him back to sleep."

"Mmm," she hums out. "That sounds perfect."

Getting up from the bed, she slips on a light pink, silk robe, cinching it around her waist. Daphne presses her lips to mine in a quick kiss, before darting out of our room and padding down the stairs.

Less than ten minutes later, I'm following in her footsteps, calling out to her. "Where are you, Little Star?"

"In the kitchen, Daddy!"

Her playful tone of voice combined with the words she purrs goes straight to my cock, and I pick up the pace until I enter the kitchen, stopping dead in my tracks.

If this is a dream, don't ever wake me up.

Daphne is perched on the kitchen island, no robe in sight and her Daddy's Girl collar in place around her neck. She's leaning back, propped up on her forearms, her knees splayed wide open, baring her pussy to me.

Ever so slowly, I stalk toward her. "Christ, woman."

I'm about to put my hands on her body, to pull her to me, but she stops me. "Wait. You had your chance this morning. Now it's my turn."

She spreads her legs a little wider, allowing me to look, but still not touch, and it's driving me mad.

"Do you see what you do to me? What you do to my body? It's all for you, Daddy, and it always will be. You took me from a little girl, and I'll always be your little girl, but you helped me transform into a more confident and loving woman, too. You've taught me patience and compassion; you've taught me to love my body—a body that I always saw as flawed. Too short, too small, too flat chested, but none of that matters when I'm with you because you worship my body, Colin."

Daphne slides forward on the counter until her legs hang over the edge. With her back flat against the granite, she runs her hands up and down her torso, cupping her breasts before rolling her nipples between her fingers.

My hands are on her thighs, pushing them even further apart, needing to see her bare. "That's because your body is perfect, baby. You're perfect."

One of her hands coasts down her body, and she slides her fingers between her legs, teasing at the folds that lay between her thighs. "But it's not just that, Daddy, is it? It's how you make me feel intelligent and precious. How you don't ask me to hide any part of myself."

A single slim finger of hers dips into her pussy, and I groan when she slowly begins to pump in and out of herself before dragging her arousal up to circle her clit. Slipping the finger back inside of her pussy, she grinds her hips against her hand. "It's how you make me feel."

I can't help myself when I slide one of my fingers inside her cunt next to her own. "Show me—show me how I make you feel."

We thrust in and out of her pussy together, slow and languid strokes. I add another finger, and she follows suit, four of our combined digits deep inside her pussy, working in tandem to bring her pleasure.

"Need you now," I manage to grunt out as my cock weeps

in my pants.

She nods but makes no move to remove her fingers. Still, I remove mine and tug down my pants. "Now, forever. You have me forever, Colin."

Somehow, I manage to climb on top of the counter without breaking a hip, thrusting inside her before she has a chance to move her fingers.

"Oh fuck, shit!"

"You okay, baby?" I ask, continuing to fuck her slowly.

"God, yes!" She purrs the words, a gentle croon that's a balm to my soul. "I feel so full this way, so stretched for you."

"Imagine what it's going to feel like when I put a plug in that ass and stretch both your holes at once."

She ruts against me, sliding her fingers out of her cunt so it's only my cock buried deep within. Rubbing her clit, she keens, a needy mewl spilling from her lips. "Don't tease me with such empty threats."

"Empty threats? Fuck no, it's a promise, Little Girl. Daddy is going to take both your holes at once, all for himself one day."

"You really are out of a romance novel, aren't you?"

I laugh, and she smiles at me, all the while we continue to move against one another. Already, I feel her beginning to clench around my shaft, her warm cunt like silk against my cock. "Does that turn you on? Thinking of me as one of the heroes of those books you're always reading in bed at night?"

"I don't need to think about you as the main character of a romance novel, Colin. I'm already living one with you by my side. Now fuck me and make me cum before BJ wakes up, and we essentially edge ourselves to death."

"It's Joseph, and whatever my Little Girl wants, my Little Girl gets."

Picking up speed, I thrust into her over and over again, my

hands slipping on the granite where I'm bracing myself over her on the cool countertop.

Daphne moans as I slide even deeper inside, hitting the spot that drives her insane. Several more long strokes and she's crying out into the kitchen, a mixture of Daddy and Colin and I love you pouring from her lips like the words of a sacred hymn as she breaks apart beneath me.

I follow her over the edge, grunting out my own release deep inside her walls, and when I pull out, I watch as if under a trance when my cum leaks from her body. Reaching out, I drag two fingers through my spent orgasm, before pushing them deep inside her.

"You are fucking primal, aren't you?" she gasps when I repeat the process.

"Daphne, you're lucky I had a vasectomy, or you would surely already be pregnant with my child. I never thought I would want another baby at my age but thinking about you round with a baby...with *my* baby...Fuck, it makes me want to get the procedure reversed and tie you to my bed where I can fuck you until you're pregnant."

Laughing, she pushes me away, but then stops, almost looking like she is searching for something. "What happens if Joseph doesn't get a forever family?"

"Well, that's not what I was expecting, but if that were to happen, a long-term foster placement would take place, where he would either remain in a foster home or he would stay in a group home with other foster kids until he ages out of the system."

She sits up, legs still dangling off the side of the counter. Daphne bites her lip, gnawing on it like she often does when she's anxious. "Do you remember the first date we went on to the steakhouse? Where we talked about a dynamic and how communication was always the biggest thing that needed to remain open at all times?"

I smile at her, remembering the day fondly. God, I was so nervous I was going to let her down. That I couldn't or wouldn't be the man she needed. "Of course I do."

"This is me keeping communication open and being vulnerable at the same time."

Sitting up next to her, I search her face. "You know you can tell me anything, always."

"What if we adopted him? I mean, if no one from his family comes forward."

Stunned, I stare at her. "You want Joseph to be part of our family forever?"

We're being as naked and bare with each other in this moment as our bodies already are—raw and exposed, dissecting and discussing our deepest desires. And it feels amazing.

"I never wanted children of my own. But that first night, hell, I was already in love with him and his little chubby cheeks before we walked out of your office. It's not me barefoot and pregnant in the kitchen, but a part of me already feels like he is ours, and I want him to have a happy life with two sisters that already love him. With a mommy and a daddy. With us. I know that it is a long process, that it can be expensive and tedious, but nothing has ever felt so right."

Looking around the kitchen, my eyes land on the clock above the oven. Not quite midnight. I press a quick kiss to her lips before jumping off the counter. "Don't you dare move. I'll be right back!"

I start to leave the kitchen, still naked and suddenly on a mission, but Daphne's voice calls out, stopping me. "Colin!"

"I'll be back in thirty seconds. I swear, Daphne, if you move an inch before I get back, I'll bend you over on that counter and spank your ass until you beg me to stop while tormenting your clit with an ice cube the entire time."

She gasps, "Daddy!"

I make it back to her in thirty-three seconds with my phone already pressed against my ear. Daphne, bad girl that she is, has shifted positions, one leg bent while the other lazily dangles over the counter. Raising an eyebrow in her direction, I bypass her to fill a glass with several cubes of ice before returning to her.

"Cynthia, I'm so sorry to wake you this late."

While Cynthia responds to my midnight pleasantries, I place Daphne's second foot back on the counter, pushing her thighs apart until she is nice and wide. I can still see my cum on the lips of her pussy, and while my mind is mostly focused on my phone call, I can't help but become momentarily spellbound as I study the place where our arousal mixes together.

"Yes," I answer Cynthia in the receiver, pulling a cube of ice from the glass and running it up one of Daphne's legs.

"No, nothing is wrong. Quite the opposite actually." I tease closer and closer to her pussy, watching as goosebumps break out across her flesh in its wake.

Finally, I dip the cube between her folds, the heat of her pussy quickly melting the ice. I circle it around and around, teasing her entrance and nearly brushing her clit as the ice cube melts, leaving a trail of cold water along Daphne's mound and through her already slick folds.

"I want to formally adopt Joseph if no other family comes forward. I already know what you're going to say—that he would do best in a dual-parent household with lots of time to commit to him, that there may be underlying trauma due to his experiences that might need treatment down the line."

This time, as I slide the ice cube up her cunt, I stop, holding it steady on her clit. She doesn't move, doesn't flinch, but the smallest of whimpers escapes. I grin at her, a bit sadistically, and continue my phone call.

"You haven't had the chance to meet her in person yet, but I'll be bringing Daphne by your office first thing on Monday morning to meet you. I'm the luckiest man alive because she agreed to marry me just this morning, and I think you will agree when we meet that she shares a very special connection with Joseph that could be beneficial for the rest of his life. Joseph will have a loving family with a mom and dad and two sisters who worship the little ground he's too young to crawl on."

Tears run down the sides of Daphne's face, and I'm not sure if it's from emotion or the extreme sensation of the ice being held against her.

"Okay, that sounds great. We'll see you then."

I hang up the phone and toss it next to us on the counter, still holding the ice cube against her flesh.

"What did she say?" she blurts out.

I shake my head at her. "Oh no, Little Girl. I'm not answering any questions until you tell me why you moved when I gave you explicit instructions not to."

Slowly, I remove my fingers from the ice cube, allowing it to fall to the counter below her ass.

"Because you left me and didn't tell me why." She squirms as the ice cube melts into nothing, a cool puddle of liquid forming beneath her.

Ready to pull her to me, to flip her over and have my way with her ass, I'm reaching for her legs when the sounds of a tiny cry echoes over the baby monitor.

We look at each other for a nanosecond before we both start laughing, a fit of giggles that ends in us each scrambling to get dressed before we chase each other up the stairs and into the room to Joseph.

Daphne beats me to his crib, gently lifting him from the

mattress as if he is a priceless antique. He soothes almost instantly under her touch, and I'm not the only one who smiles when we notice it. As she holds him, I hold her, my arms wrapped around her body. And she's right, so perfectly right as she always is.

He already is ours.

Epilogue

DAPHNE

Eighteen Months Later

ALL AROUND THE BACKYARD, BALLOONS FLOAT GENTLY IN the warm June breeze, tethered to the deck and the backs of chairs. A large folding table is covered in a shimmery, rainbow tablecloth—my pick for the occasion, thank you—non-traditional pink and blue outdated gender roles, and there is enough food spread across its surface to feed the entirety of the state of North Carolina.

Family and friends tumble out through the house and into the yard. Not a mixture of my friends and Colin's friends, but truly our friends.

Our *family*.

Earlier this week, we finalized the process of adoption, finally bringing Joseph home while knowing no one will ever be able to tear him away from us. It was a long, often brutal process filled with questionnaires and home studies, countless packets of paperwork and endless sleepless nights.

Many of those nights, I cried, acutely aware that there was a very real possibility that he could be taken away from us. It was a constant ache in my chest that I could never quite diminish, even as we grew more and more confident that the adoption would be successful.

"Mama, up!" a little voice coos at my feet, grabby hands out and waiting for liftoff.

Scooping Joseph into my arms, hearing him call me Mama as I nuzzle his little face and inhale his clean, baby scent—it's a feeling I never thought I wanted, but nowadays, I wonder how I ever lived without it.

It's amazing how much he's grown in what feels like such a short time, blossoming from this little, helpless babe into essentially a tiny drunk person who is always stumbling his way around the big world in front of him, hell-bent on doing things on his own. He points to everything, loves the word *no* more than a playful brat antagonizing her Dom, and even uses a fork when he feeds himself.

Colin makes his way across the deck, placing a full platter of burgers and hot dogs onto the already crowded surface before crossing over to where I stand with our son.

He drops a quick kiss on my lips before dropping one on the top of Joseph's head, and the simple contact is still enough to bring me to my knees. "You doing okay, baby? This is a hell of a lot more people than I expected to show up."

"Me too, and it's your turn to drop some change into the swear jar now." I giggle back, so deeply filled with gratitude for all the people here today to celebrate our family.

"Think we can sneak away for a minute?" he asks while nuzzling into my neck. "I have a surprise that's just for you."

My eyes light up, loving every surprise this man has ever given me. Like when he surprised me the night he pushed me up against the wall and almost kissed me, the day he rounded me in the kitchen, placing gentle kisses on every design permanently etched onto my skin, the day he confessed his love to me and proposed to me all while I had baby puke on my shirt.

Looking around the yard, I see Emily and Laurel—the daughters I never knew I needed. Because much like Joseph, who didn't come from me physically, they are all my children, and I will protect them until the day I die.

My eyes scan further to Mina and Nico where they stand together, his hand placed protectively on her swollen, pregnant belly. Around a table, Pauli sits, chatting animatedly with Tabitha's parents, who graciously and excitedly accepted our invitation to join our celebration. I've met the couple on a few occasions over the last year and a half and was not only welcomed into their home with open arms, but into their family, too.

Lawyers from Colin's office mingle with our crew from Broken Sparrow, the dichotomy between the two professions taking an almost comical approach. Still, it isn't lost on me when I notice Raven chatting up a young paralegal that Colin's office recently hired.

Get it, girl.

Giving me a little squeeze, Colin nudges me toward the sliding door that leads back into the house. "Come on, five minutes. He'll be fine."

Yeah, maybe I have just a *bit* of separation anxiety when it comes to leaving Joseph behind. I just never want to let him out of my sight, the underlying fear of him being taken from us not completely gone. "Fine, but I'm not going to be happy about it."

We swing by the table, dropping our son into Pauli's waiting arms. She immediately begins fussing over him, planting kisses all over his still chubby cheeks while I smooth his dark hair. "Mama and Daddy will be right back, BJ."

Colin groans at the endearment. "Are you ever going to stop calling him that?"

Bumping his hip with mine, I playfully respond, "Yeah, when you stop calling shit-filled diapers *polluted poopers*."

"What else do you expect me to call them, Daphne? Disgusting doodies? Shit swaddlers? Acrid ass covers?"

I roll my eyes, groaning while pushing him away from me. Over the last year and a half, he's grown into a man full of so much light. He laughs and jokes with all of us, like when he still relentlessly teases me when I dry heave changing a diaper or when he teases our daughters over their crushes of the week. "You're such a freaking dad."

He pulls me into his arms, growling into my ear so no one else can hear him. "I may be a dad, Little Star, but don't forget that the same man you are making fun of is also your Daddy. And you love your Daddy and his cock, don't you?"

One thing that hasn't changed though? He still has a delightfully flithy mouth.

We cross the threshold into the house, Colin's hands already at my sides, tickling me relentlessly. Before the door shuts, we hear someone call out, "Don't do anything we wouldn't do," and it quickly sends us both into a fit of laughter.

He pushes me toward the office, but I stop him with my hands on his chest. "I have something for you, too. I need to get it from upstairs."

Less than a minute later, I enter the office and close the door behind me, meeting my husband's steady gaze with an adoring smile on my face.

Because that's another thing that has changed in the last year and a half.

Colin and I were engaged for three full days before we decided to make it official. While we talked about a traditional wedding, we both felt it was best if we went into the adoption process already legally bound, allowing us to adopt Joseph together as opposed to a single-parent adoption.

It was a small and intimate affair, held right in our backyard —just us, our three children, his mother, sister, and Nico.

Oh, and Stella.

"Come here and let me give you your surprise," he rasps, breaking my daydream.

I round the desk and sit on the solid wooden surface, Colin spreading his muscular thighs to give me room. With a raised brow, I ask, "What did I do to deserve a surprise?"

"You were born." He pulls a black box from a drawer on the side of his desk. "You came into my life." Colin slides the lid open to reveal a dainty, silver bar attached to a chain. "You made me want to live again." He lifts the necklace from the box and presents it to me so I can see the three stones embedded across the bar. One stone glints in the light for each of our children in their accompanying birthstone. "You made me a father again when it was something I didn't even know I wanted." Turning the bar over, he shows me the engraving scrawled across the back that reads *Daddy's Little Star*. "You made me remember how good it feels to love someone and to be loved by someone."

Colin stands, gently sweeping my hair behind my shoulder before clasping the necklace around my neck. Much in the way he did the first night he placed my Daddy's Girl collar around my neck. Much in the way he still places beautiful collars of different colors and materials around my neck when we engage in the special type of play we both love and have continued to explore together.

I finger the necklace, running my fingers over the stones, and loving that I have a secret message from him that I'll be able to keep against my skin every day. My eyes well up, my tears threatening to spill over. "Thank you doesn't feel like enough, but I do have something for you, too."

Still sitting on the desk, I wriggle to reach into my pocket, holding the item inside my closed fist. "You've given me more than I ever could have dreamed possible. You made me a wife and a mother, and I know that it wasn't an easy journey for you. I also know that there is one person to thank, that without her, I wouldn't have you as the caring man and fucking phenomenal father that you are."

Gesturing for his right hand, I slowly slide the ring onto his right index finger, watching his face as he registers the smooth, metal band.

"How did you..." he trails off in astonishment, unable to finish his sentence.

Colin has no idea that I've been holding onto this ring for over a year, been waiting for the exact moment to give it back to him.

"I had taken the girls to visit Tabitha's final resting place last year shortly after you and I divulged our relationship to them. I wanted them to know I was there for them, that I was there to be their fiercest ally and deepest confidant but that I still wanted to respect their relationship with her. At first, I gave them time to be with their mom, standing off to the side and giving them space, but quickly, they asked me to come sit with them so I did. I sat between my girls, listening to them talk to the woman who gave birth to them, the woman who raised them until it was my turn to take over where she left off. When it was time to go, I pushed up from the ground, and the sunlight reflected on something in front of Tabitha's headstone.It was only when I looked toward the shimmer that I saw your ring sitting on the ground."

Without using words, he lifts me from the desk, my legs wrapping around his sturdy torso. Colin's lips crash against mine in kisses filled with urgent devotion and desire as his arms cradle me steadily against his body.

We pull apart, panting with kiss-swollen lips. I cup his face with both my hands, rubbing over his scruffy yet defined jaw. "She's part of our story, Colin."

He stares into my eyes with reverence and tears full of new promises and beginnings. Rasping against my lips, between kisses, he growls out, "Then let's get writing, baby, because we've got a hell of a lot more story ahead of us."

THE END

Author's Note

If I'm being honest, when I first decided to write Colin and Daphne's story, I was beyond apprehensive. It wasn't a story I was looking forward to and I was worried I wouldn't be able to work my twisted sense of humor into its pages while tackling such serious topics. But as I began to develop these two characters, I learned quickly that they would be two of my favorites to date.

Throughout the story, Colin and Daphne worked through grief —sometimes in constructive ways and sometimes in not so constructive ways—that brought them each to a place where they could freely express love to others once again. And while my own journey with grief is vastly different from both of the characters in Etched, there is a very personal story weaved within their journey—a journey that I still struggle with on a daily basis. A journey I'm sure many others have experienced too.

I would be amiss if I didn't take a moment to acknowledge the pain and suffering that accompanies grief, and I would be equally untoward if I didn't take a moment to introduce you to a dear friend of mine who not only experienced grief much like

Colin did throughout Etched, but who has turned overcoming grief into her life's calling.

While Kari and I have only had the pleasure of meeting in person once, I have followed along on her journey for many years—from her years as a video editor to her current passion as a grief and widow coach. I have turned to her in my time of need, have relied on her kind words more times than I can count, and have laughed out loud at the stories she tells openly of her family.

Part of the inspiration behind Etched, Kari has shown me time and time again what it means to move forward while keeping the memory of your loved ones close and I know she can do the same for you.

Don't struggle alone in grief.

https://karidriskell.com

Acknowledgments

To every single person who had a hand in making Etched come alive, I truly mean it when I say that I couldn't have done it without you.

My brilliant wife—it's still so freaking cool to be able to call you that--thank you for putting up with all my crazy ideas. For never getting mad when I wake you up in the middle of the night to run plot points with you, and for always being the first person to read each chapter as it's written.

Tiffany, my amazing editor—thank you for always getting my comma usage under control, for cracking me up with your notes (team peanut butter pie!), and for helping me to polish each and every manuscript I throw your way.

The badass duo of Cady and Tori that make up Cruel Ink Editing + Design—I don't think a day will ever come where I am not in awe of the talent you both possess. From each cover, to countless graphics, and phenomenal formatting, you both knock it out of the park with each and every project.

And of course, to all my alphas, betas, ARC readers, and Street Team. The effort you put into everything you do never goes unnoticed! Thank you for every post you share or create, every minute you spend on awesome TikToks, every review, and each bit of feedback you give me along the way.

Other Works

About The Author

Amity Malcom was born in Pennsylvania. She began writing short stories while still in elementary school-including a total page turner about how her mother loved to fish. Her mother does not love to fish and is actually terrified by ocean creatures.

She now resides in Florida with her wife, two completely insane but lovable cats and one neurotic but adorable dog.

When not writing steamy characters and happily ever afters, Amity can be found watching professional soccer, exploring Florida's many theme parks, and campaigning for LGBTQIA+ rights.

www.ingramcontent.com/pod-product-compliance
Lightning Source LLC
Chambersburg PA
CBHW071433260626
47170CB00008B/2694